Merrily bit her lower lip pensively.

Did he find her beautiful? With a sigh, she shook her head at her reflection.

She wasn't Merrily Knight anymore; she was Merrily Butler. Mrs. Garth Butler. She frowned at the finely chiseled bones of her oval face, the dimple in her strong, determined chin. Don't let me lose you again, Garth.

She should have told Garth sooner that they would have to call off their honeymoon trip to Aspen. She would have if she'd known.

More than anything, Merrily wanted their marriage to work. She wanted them to be a real family. But Garth was holding back. Something was bothering him, something more important than missing the chance to honeymoon in a remote cabin in the mountains.

Thoughts and reflections on her wedding, earlier that afternoon, enveloped her. From early morning on, her entire day marched before her as she tried to figure out what had gone wrong.

FOR ALWAYS

Molly Noble Bull

Serenade/Serenata
BOOKS
of the Zondervan Publishing House
Grand Rapids, Michigan

A Note From the Author:
*I love to hear from my readers! You may correspond with me by
writing:*

> Molly Noble Bull
> 1415 Lake Drive, S.E.
> Grand Rapids, MI 49506

FOR ALWAYS
Copyright © 1986 by Molly Noble Bull

Serenade/Serenata is an imprint of Zondervan Publishing House,
1415 Lake Drive, S.E., Grand Rapids, Michigan 49506.

ISBN 0-310-47352-7

Edited by Anne Severance
Designed by Kim Koning

Printed in the United States of America

86 87 88 89 90 91 / 10 9 8 7 6 5 4 3 2 1

Dedication

To my husband, Charlie Bull, to our three sons and my parents. And to Peggy Cleaves and Patti Boeckman, the two best friends a new writer could hope for. But to God give the glory.

CHAPTER 1

"Why didn't you tell me we were going to have to cancel our honeymoon trip, Merrily?"

Stunned, Merrily peered up at her husband of almost three hours, groping for an answer, but no words came. A haunting hurt lurked behind Garth Butler's dark, expressive eyes. He'd never looked at her quite like that before. It tore her heart to see it. She'd wronged him somehow, and she sensed that it was more than the cancellation of their trip to Colorado.

"I was looking forward to two weeks alone with you in Aspen," he went on, hiding the hurt behind lowered black lashes, "whether you were or not."

"But I was!" she exclaimed fervently, her blue eyes pleading for understanding. "Surely you know that."

"Frankly, I'm not entirely certain what I believe."

The deep timbre in his voice never failed to excite her, even now when it was tinged with resentment.

7

He opened the door to their motel room and gestured for her to go inside.

Her pulse racing, Merrily preceded him into the cool luxury of the gold and white bridal suite, afraid even to look back for fear of finding that Garth wasn't following. The hum of the air conditioning unit sounded strangely in tune with her pounding heart. She stepped restlessly across the plush, gold carpet, gripping the small, white patent leather purse she was carrying with long, nervous fingers.

She could hear him moving behind her, slamming down their overnight bags on the wooden bench at the end of the king-size bed, then emitting a loud exhalation of breath when he'd finished. She had to do something, engage herself in some sort of busy work, or she would go mad.

Nervously, she unpinned the white, rose corsage from the lapel of her blue crepe jacket and surveyed the room in search of something to put the roses in. It was ridiculous to worry about flowers at such a time, but Merrily always involved herself in trivia when she was upset.

Still shaking, she glanced back at Garth. "If you'll excuse me, I want to put my corsage in water."

"No problem, I was on my way out to the car to get the rest of our things anyway." She heard brisk footfalls, then the door banged shut.

Stalking across the carpet in the direction of the dressing room toward the back, she was aware of the feel of her high-heeled white sandals crunching into the thick pile as if snuffing him under . . . and thus out of her mind. But she would never erase the memory of his pained, black eyes. Even now, when he'd left the room, they haunted her . . . piercing her inner being.

Tears washed her large sapphire blue eyes, highlighting her rare beauty. She couldn't stand the

8

thought of hurting someone, especially Garth.

She stared down at the clear, glass ashtray on the counter next to the sink for a moment, catching her breath. With trembling fingers, she filled the ashtray with water and carefully put the corsage in it. Satisfied, she glanced up at her own image in the mirror above the dressing counter and pushed back a stray, near-black curl that escaped the tight coil of her French twist.

Merrily bit her full, lower lip pensively. Did he find her beautiful? With a sigh, she shook her head at her reflection. *My face is okay, I guess,* she thought, examining her flawless, olive skin with narrowed eyes. *Too much cheekbone though and I need more color.* She opened her purse, removed a compact of tawny-rose blusher and applied it to her soft, well-tanned cheeks.

She wasn't Merrily Knight anymore; she was Merrily Butler. Mrs. Garth Butler. She frowned at the finely chiseled bones of her oval face, the dimple in her strong, determined chin. *Don't let me lose you again, Garth.*

She should have told Garth sooner that they would have to call off the Aspen trip. She would have if she'd known. What was her mother doing changing a light globe three hours before her wedding in the first place?

More than anything, Merrily wanted their marriage to work. She wanted them, along with Todd and Suzan, to be a real family. But Garth was holding back. Something was bothering him, something more important than missing the chance to honeymoon in a remote cabin in the mountains.

Having repaired her makeup, Merrily removed the matching jacket to her blue crepe outfit. The V neck dress underneath was simply styled and complimented her face and figure. She wanted Garth to see her at her best. *Anything* to make things right again.

Thoughts and reflections on her wedding, earlier that afternoon, enveloped her. From early morning on, her entire day marched before her as she tried to figure out what had gone wrong.

It had been a hot, Houston afternoon in late July. Merrily's retired army father, Ronald Manning, arrived early in order to drive Merrily and her two children to the hospital to visit her mother before going all the way across town to the little chapel where Merrily and Garth were to exchange their vows. During their brief visit, her mother must have apologized a hundred times for backing out after promising to keep Todd and Suzan while they honeymooned.

The unfortunate fall from the ladder and the resulting broken ankle had cancelled any chance they had of her mother keeping Merrily's children. Her father agreed to keep them on their wedding night but didn't feel confident enough to babysit them for two weeks. Garth's family flew back to North Dakota immediately after the reception.

She'd just unfastened the last pearl button and was folding her jacket across a high, straight-backed chair in front of the counter when she heard Garth directly behind her. She smelled the scent of pipe tobacco, then saw his darkly handsome face in the mirror. Almost shyly, she averted her eyes from his. Was she playing the bashful virgin? Pretending to be the girl he knew seven years ago?

Something happened during the interim since flashing her that pained expression only minutes before. Garth had softened. She saw that in the brief moment when their eyes caught. Maybe he had forgiven her for not telling him sooner about her mother's fall.

Everything happened so quickly. One minute she was dressing for her wedding, the next she was visiting her mother in the hospital. It was a wonder she made it to the chapel on time.

"Merrily," he said gently and in that deep, heart-melting voice again. "I'm sorry. I shouldn't have gotten so upset."

Looking up, he caught her gaze and held it. He was the Garth she remembered. Charming. Caring. Romantic. The fire in his black eyes, his vibrant smile, transformed her. She had no desire to glance away.

"Did you notice Todd and Suzan at the reception?" he asked, while his bold gaze asked an entirely different question. "They were all over the place, weren't they? Sampling all the refreshments, playing with the white streamers you gave them, tooting those silly, paper horns. They're sweet kids, Merrily. You've done a good job. But did you notice how they looked at us when I kissed you after the ceremony? I don't think they liked it a bit."

"They were probably embarrassed," she rationalized. "Don't you think?"

"I hope you're right," he said, but she didn't think he was entirely convinced.

His mesmerizing gaze dropped from the blue of her eyes to her upturned mouth and stayed there. She trembled in response.

"And are you aware that you introduced my Uncle Ted as Uncle Tom at the reception?" His dark eyes danced. "But don't worry about it. He said you were a charmer." His deep tone was gentle. Mesmerizing. Sending waves of stirring emotion through her. "And I couldn't agree more."

"Did I actually call him Uncle Tom?" His gaze rippled across the intimate space between them. "Really?" she asked.

11

He nodded teasingly. "Really."

Merrily felt foolish. Her blushing cheeks showed it. He had already discovered her problem, the nervous habit. Her desire to appear mysterious went sailing out the door. His mere presence disarmed her. "Sometimes I say names wrong," she explained finally in a soft, shaky voice. "Especially when I'm nervous."

He flashed concern. "Are you nervous now?"

She wanted to say yes. But somehow his caring expression relaxed her as no tranquilizer ever could.

When he saw her smile, his eyes twinkled mischievously.

"Why Captain Butler!" A whimsically shocked expression curved her lips. "You're not playing fair."

He grinned sheepishly. "Now why would you say a thing like that?"

The playful grin broadened, starting in his eyes and spreading all over his handsome face. His dark brown suit hugged his broad shoulders, trim waist, and narrow hips to perfection. His straight, soldier's body was hard and muscled. She longed to feel his strong arms around her, run her fingers through his thick, curly, black hair.

This was to be their only night alone without Todd and Suzan. The next morning they would pick up the children, stop by the hospital for one last visit with her parents, and board a jet for Germany and a new life.

She knew that if she hoped to capture his heart until death parted them, she would have to do it before they changed from "couple" to "family." At best, it would be difficult. It wouldn't be easy for a thirtyish bachelor to take on all three of them at once without problems, and she knew it. Too many of her friends failed at just that task.

12

"Cap'n," she said at last in a low, whispery voice. "I do believe you're flirting with me."

"Ma'am, I do believe you're right."

His dark eyes mirrored his amused smile. They exchanged perceptive glances for a brief instant and then they were laughing.

The O'Hara/Butler thing was a game they'd been playing since the first summer they met. She was fourteen then to Garth's twenty-two. Merrily had been fascinated with her father's new protégé, a tall, darkly handsome, second lieutenant with an intriguing last name. She'd been reading *Gone With the Wind* and saw a connection between "Butler the hero" and "Butler the army officer." And she still did.

Merrily was blushing after the laughter faded. Even that was discarded as she curved her slender arms around his neck and glanced up into his dark eyes. The magic that flashed between them was both stirring and sweet. Her long lashes lowered, her full lips turned up in a brilliant smile.

She wanted him to kiss her, hold her. For one brief moment she forgot the children, and that she had not seen him in seven years until three days before the wedding and hardly knew him. Slowly her blue gaze traveled across the wide expanse of his chest and lingered on his tender, sculptured lips.

He was devouring her with his eyes, but an undercurrent of tenderness endeavored to shine through. The love she saw was glorious. How she had dreamed of this moment during their years of separation. Never in their three-year marriage had Mark Knight ever made her feel as she felt in Garth's melting embrace.

He reached for the stray curl that dropped from her carefully groomed hair, and breathed in the enchanting scent almost reverently. Unhurried, he

13

allowed the curl to wind around his forefinger for a moment. Finally, he let it drop to the sleeve of her blue silk dress. He watched it tremble there a moment as his lips slowly softened.

Merrily's heart caught in her throat. She could hear his breathing when he removed the rest of the hair pins, one by one, his sharp intake of breath when he had finished. Unrestrained, her thick, dark mane fell, down her back to settle several inches below her tiny waist.

The magnetic pull of his gaze drew her to him, and she had no wish to be freed from it. He savored the curving trimness of her form while running long, bold fingers through the dark depths of her hair. His black eyes whispered sweet, love words that his lips would never utter.

He pulled her to him. His mouth claimed hers in a kiss of demanding passion, filling her senses with only him.

"Darling," he moaned into her hair.

He lifted her tenderly into his arms and carried her to the bed. The love that they expressed for each other took her breath away.

A peace fell upon Merrily then, wrapping her in the warmth of commitment to Garth and their marriage and to the new family they would become. She rested her dark head on his broad shoulder, her mouth turned up in a smile.

Much later, Merrily crossed to the French doors, nursing a cup of steaming coffee, and pulled the curtain cord. The white drape rustled softly as it glided across the heavy brass rod to reveal a well-tended expanse of green grass and towering pines. Garth joined her; both wore the blue terry cloth robes she had purchased at Foley's the week before.

"Wake up, lazybones!" she scolded playfully, tossing her head so that her thick mane cascaded across his chest in a tickling caress.

"Cut that out, Merrily!" He laughed. "I mean it!"

"Your wife's starving!"

"But your husband's sleepy." He took her coffee, set it on a nearby lamp table, and pulled her to him for a quick but tender kiss. When he released her he said, "Can't we skip dinner and have two tomorrow night?"

Pretending outrage, Merrily jerked away. "Skip dinner? Never!" Teasingly, she tossed her head, spilling her hair across one shoulder. "And if we don't go right now, all the best restaurants will be closed, and I refuse to eat in a fast-food restaurant on my wedding night." She cast him a flirtatious smile. "Lands sakes, Cap'n, I'm darn near starved."

"You're very persuasive, ma'am." He traced her lips with his long forefinger, then he reached for her again, pulling her to him. "I think maybe you've got yourself a deal."

Merrily shivered in response to his tickling breath on her neck as he whispered into her hair.

"Tell me," he said, "did Mark have this problem, too? Or did you have other ways of persuading him?"

Merrily stiffened, seething with indignation. Why did he have to bring up her late husband now? Instantly, she moved away from him, shivering with emotion.

"That was a cheap shot I just made, Merrily." Garth's handsome face held an expression of sincerity she couldn't ignore. "I don't even know why I said it." His black eyes begged for understanding. "You'll never know how sorry I am."

She desperately wanted to give him the understanding he needed at that moment, but she felt drained. Empty. All she could think of was getting away from the tortured pull of his eyes. But she

15

couldn't move.

Why was he staring at her so intently? What was he thinking? She dragged her gaze from his and looked down at her shaking hands. Did he expect her to forget what he had said and just fall into his arms? If only it were that simple.

Garth studied her unblinkingly. Why hadn't she accepted his sincere apology? Granted, his outburst was indefensible, but he had tried to make amends, hadn't he? What more could he possibly say?

The pain so apparent in his dark gaze was clearly destroying her. Merrily swallowed. She had to be alone if only for a minute.

"I think I'll take a shower now," she said, still trembling after the long silence. "Then we can go out to eat, if you still want to."

"Of course I still want to."

She should have accepted his apology right then instead of standing there frozen and tongue-tied. But no words came. He just kept appraising her as if they were engaged in some sort of nonverbal conversation. They were, but she didn't want to acknowledge it.

Merrily forced herself to turn away before she started to cry. She had blown it. One chance to begin their marriage on solid ground before the children entered the picture, and she had destroyed it.

Or *was* it her fault? He was the one who brought up Mark. Still, she should have forgiven him. With a heavy heart, she slipped into the bathroom and turned on the tap.

In Mark's arms she had dreamed of Garth, then hated herself for doing it. Was she being punished now? She had Garth's name, but he had never really mentioned love . . .

Merrily's slender, shapely body tingled as the warm spray of water caressed her delicate skin. Yet it wasn't the shower that excited her; it was the memory of Garth's strong arms holding her, his tender kiss engulfing her with a passion that was beyond her wildest dreams. Even now as the remembrance of his love was still new, still fresh, she wondered why she agreed to marry him so hastily. She didn't usually make rash decisions. Her mother had pointed that out to her more than once lately.

"You know how your father and I love Garth," her mother had said. "Why, he's like a son to us. But you haven't seen him in ages, honey. You say you should have married him instead of Mark. Well, I'm not saying that maybe you aren't right. Your Dad and I both saw it coming. The looks you two exchanged were enough to convince me. But nevertheless, you married Mark. And even though you and Garth have been corresponding these last few months, you haven't seen him for years. People change, honey. He's not the man you knew then. He couldn't be. And you're not the girl he knew either. This just isn't like you, Merrily. Can't you see that?"

And she could see, but it didn't change the way she felt about Garth. She knew it never would.

He'd proposed by mail. Before the mad correspondence started, she'd not seen Garth Butler since that Christmas at the lake.

Everybody was surprised when he accepted her parents' invitation. It seemed unlikely that Garth would decide to spend Christmas with the Manning family at their cottage on a lake west of San Antonio, Texas, when he had a mother and father in North Dakota.

Her parents bought the property when her father was stationed at Fort Sam Houston, and they moved there permanently after her father retired. But *that* Christmas, she remembered, her father was still very much a soldier. When Garth arrived, he'd closeted Garth in his study for endless hours of what Dad called "men talk." She'd hardly seen Garth those first few days and missed terribly their usual, witty exchanges.

On Garth's third afternoon there Merrily took a walk along the lake. The sky was bleak and threatening. A cold wind was at her back.

She shivered a little because she had been too stubborn to wear her heavy coat as her mother suggested. She wore only jeans and a white pullover sweater. Suddenly she felt somebody watching her. Looking up, she saw Garth for the first time, not as a family friend but as a very desirable man. Strange stirrings, like nothing she had experienced before, flooded her senses and shocked her a little. She knew that she should turn away. Run. But she couldn't.

She had reminded herself that she was already engaged to Mark Knight. He was expected to arrive for a visit in less than two weeks to finalize their wedding plans. Yet she couldn't ignore the obvious. Garth caught and held her blue eyes with his black gaze for a sweet eternity. She would remember the way his broad shoulders filled the tan brush jacket and those smoldering black eyes for the rest of her life.

"I have to go," she had said, after a long silence, and started back toward the house. He stopped her, held her. Their eyes fused again in an even more startling exchange. "Garth! I'm engaged."

He ignored her, his lips moving ever closer to hers. She was wild from wanting his kiss by the time their lips finally touched.

His kiss was deep and searing. She felt weak and trembly but passionately elated, more alive than she had ever felt before.

"That wasn't the kiss of a girl who's in love with someone else," he said when he had released her. He hesitated, as if waiting for her to deny what he had said. When she didn't, he continued. "My brother, Roger, is very ill in North Dakota. I just got word, and I have to leave right away. But I'll be back for you, Merrily. Don't marry Mark."

But she hadn't waited. How could she? One quick kiss and goodbye without another word. By the time Mark arrived on New Year's Eve, she had made up her mind to forget Garth and marry Mark as planned.

That morning, as the postman arrived, something told her she had a letter from Garth. She almost flew to the mailbox. The brief card read, *Merrily. Roger is much better, and I'll see you in three or four days. Wait for me. Garth.* He had not written so much as a "love Garth" on that lousy card, and she hated him for making her wish that he had. There was nothing in the brief note to make her chance cancelling her future for . . . just a few empty words.

So she married Mark Knight.

Though in Mark's arms she never once felt the way she had felt in those brief, magic moments with Garth, she was happy. How could she be otherwise with a handsome husband who loved her and two beautiful children all in three years? Then Mark was gone, killed in an accident on the freeway on the way to his job as an engineer for a large oil company.

She was lost. Drained. She had never been at such a low point. Yet she had to pretend otherwise for the sake of her children.

She didn't hear from Garth at the time of Mark's death. Three years later when her parents were touring Europe, they ran into him in Munich and told him what had happened.

Merrily and the children had stayed on in Houston in order to be near her retired parents in San Antonio. She was baffled and more than a little thrilled when she got a long, newsy letter from Captain Garth Butler who was stationed in Volksheim, West Germany. She read it over and over until the pages wore thin.

She'd known, even before she opened his letter, that if Garth ever asked her to marry him, she would. Nothing would keep her from him this time.

Now she wondered. Maybe her mother was right. Maybe she had been too hasty in accepting Garth's proposal. She was still wondering the next morning as Garth drove her to her old apartment to pick up her children and belongings in readiness for the transcontinental flight.

They turned right after leaving the Katy Freeway. Several blocks down she spotted a small, white-painted church near a shopping center. A flood of memories captured her. She always dropped her children off at Sunday school, but she hadn't attended a Sunday service since . . . since she left home at eighteen for Austin, the University of Texas, and a major in education.

A family that prays together, stays together, the sign in front of the church read. Did Garth pray? She doubted it. He simply wasn't the type. With a sigh, she squelched the thought and peered down the pine banked street ahead.

Garth watched Merrily's reaction to the church with interest but said nothing. He'd often wondered what her views were on the subject. It just never came up. As a child, faith in God was very important to him, his only link to the mother he never knew.

On those occasions when he was allowed to visit with his real mother's brother, Ted Thomas, he learned that his mother had been a devout Christian. In a feeble attempt to be like her, Garth attended church services with his uncle whenever he visited him. Monique, Garth's stepmother, was not a churchgoer nor did she encourage her children to be.

"That may be one reason that Monique and your father have never gotten along," Garth's uncle, Ted Thomas, often said. "A strong faith in God is the glue that keeps marriages together."

But Garth had other ideas as to what his marriage to Merrily needed in order to survive. They needed that closeness that can only be found when a couple are truly alone. Somehow, he'd have to get Merrily to agree to go on leave with him once they got to Germany. Garth glanced briefly away from the wheel in order to look at his bride.

Merrily dazzled his senses every time she moved into his line of vision, and that moment was no exception. He'd wanted her for seven years. No. He wanted Merrily even before that Christmas in Texas. Now he could assume that she wanted him. She agreed to wed him. But she'd wanted Mark *more*, had chosen Mark over him. Garth was convinced that she still loved her late husband.

Was he jealous? The idea appalled him. It sounded too childish to actually consider. But he knew he'd resent *any* man that so much as looked at Merrily.

When they met, she had just been Major Manning's beautiful, young daughter, but a well-developed child, he remembered, for fourteen. That was his first summer on active duty after a May graduation from West Point. He'd been flattered when the Major took a special interest in him, asked him to his quarters to meet Mrs. Manning and Merrily.

Three years later when Merrily was seventeen, however, he really began to take a personal interest

21

in her. The Mannings were stationed at Fort Sam Houston, Texas, then; he was at Fort Dix. He'd planned to stop by San Antonio for a brief visit before flying on to North Dakota for the remainder of his leave. After seeing Merrily again, Garth ended up spending two weeks with the Mannings.

Merrily didn't know of his growing interest. How could she? He'd kept things strictly casual. She was still in high school. He couldn't afford to mess up her future by wooing her prematurely. Besides, she was involved in school affairs and had a steady boyfriend.

Garth couldn't remember his name. Steve something-or-other. Garth would probably have been jealous of the kid if he hadn't known that the Major was expecting a transfer of orders momentarily.

After that visit Garth corresponded with Merrily off and on for two years, all friendly, "no strings" letters that delighted him. It was Mrs. Manning that invited him to spend Christmas with the family on that memorable occasion seven years ago, and he promptly accepted. He knew he'd hurt his kid brother, Roger, by not accepting his parents' invitation instead. But he *had* to see Merrily again, try to talk her out of marrying Mark. If only it had worked.

Lately, he wondered if he was losing his perspective where Merrily was concerned. He wanted every part of her. Not merely her body. He wanted that inner layer that Mark still occupied, that undefinable essence that so eluded him.

Somehow, he felt less of a man for wanting her so desperately. He was even becoming fond of Mark's children.

Mark's children, he thought, and a muscle tightened in his firm, square jaw. *They should have been my kids; they would have been if* . . . briefly he shut his eyes. Did Merrily guess what he'd been thinking?

Was that why she refused to accept his apology? Did she know how empty he felt? Or did she care?

She'd made it clear that Mark was a forbidden topic of discussion. He could only surmise that Mark's children were also off limits. He was unsure exactly what his relationship to her children should be. But he was fairly certain that "fathering" was not part of it. They had a father, Mark.

He was still thinking those thoughts when the blonde behind the KLM ticket desk at the airport broke into his reflections later that morning. She'd surprised him a little, he recalled, because her blue eyes were the exact color of Merrily's. He liked her instantly.

"May I help you, sir?" she said in a slight, Western European accent.

"Yes, please," he replied after a long, embarrassing pause. "I have a reservation for four on flight 472. Two adults and two children. The name's Butler. Captain G. A. Butler.

"Oh, yes, Captain Butler. Here you are, flight 472. That will be . . ."

Garth handed her his VISA card as soon as she quoted the cost of the one-way flights. The flight for two to Aspen, he remembered, had been cancelled, and he wondered if Merrily would have so easily cancelled her honeymoon with Mark.

One night at a Houston motel could hardly be called a honeymoon. But it was all they'd had, all they would have for weeks . . . maybe months. His only hope rested in Merrily's ability to make new friends quickly, a skill she was forced to acquire as an army brat. If she met another woman she trusted, she might consent to leave the children with her for a week or two while they went on leave somewhere. On leave and alone, he'd court her as she should have been courted before they married. Otherwise, his chances looked rather dim.

"Your tickets, sir." The blonde ticket seller tore through the thick haze of conflicting thoughts again and most successfully. He returned her smile. "And have a nice flight, sir."

"Thank you."

Garth had managed to book a commercial jet flight for four to Amsterdam via KLM, Royal Dutch Airlines, rather than waiting for space available on an army plane. There was no use staying in Houston now that their honeymoon plans had been aborted. At Merrily's request, they booked a special, conventional aircraft from Amsterdam in order to fly low over the Netherlands. She'd read of the unique flight in a travel magazine and thought it would be exciting for the children. They would leave Houston International, have a layover in Montreal that included a long wait and refueling, and touch down in Amsterdam the next morning. From there they would fly to Frankfurt and go by train to Volksheim on the Main River where they would make their home.

The long series of flights were especially exhausting for the children. Todd and Suzan were sleeping when they dipped over Holland. Merrily never enjoyed anything more. From the air, all of Holland looked like a page from *Hans Brinker* with tiny trees and windmills, green pastures, and tiny patches of color here and there edging the famous dikes. She couldn't hide her excitement. She felt self-conscious, flushed, as Garth watched her with an expression of amused enthrallment. The long-awaited landing in Frankfurt, West Germany, was almost a letdown after Holland. Jet lag and two fussy children didn't help. By the time they'd reached the hotel, their problems had multiplied. Yet strangely, Garth felt playful.

After carrying both Suzan and Todd across the threshold, he swept Merrily into his arms and carried her across to the tune of laughter provided by her two, young children. Her crisp, musical laugh blended smoothly with Garth's deep, heartwarming chuckle. The look that crossed between them at that moment slowly deepened. Something quite different, compelling, surfaced, briefly stopping her breathing.

Their bags and other gear were still outside the door in the absence of a proper bellhop, but in Garth's arms, Merrily wasn't thinking about baggage. Just as their lips moved close for the kiss Merrily so wanted, she heard a noise outside in the hall. Her lips were only inches from Garth's, but she pulled away and glanced toward the door. Todd and Suzan were attempting to lift the largest of the four big suitcases and making a loud, scraping sound while doing it. Other hotel guests would surely complain about the noise if she didn't stop them.

Garth followed her gaze and shrugged teasingly. "How about letting Uncle Garth help you two with those bags," he said, surprising Merrily with the new term, *Uncle Garth*.

He'd not referred to himself in that way until that instant. The children had been calling him Mr. Butler or merely Captain. Merrily was thoughtful for a moment. *Uncle* noted a close relationship, perhaps a good one, but it didn't mean father. Was it Garth's way of telling her that he never intended to be a father to her children? She swallowed, then, and mentally counted to ten. She had to stop torturing herself with her fears and constant doubts. It could wreck her marriage before it actually started.

Still gathering her thoughts, she watched as Garth put down the suitcases, side by side on the oak bench near the bed. He touched his spine, feigning an aching back, then went back for the yellow

25

wooden toybox.

He dropped it to the brown carpet with a soft thud and glanced comically at Merrily. She couldn't help laughing in spite of her concerns. He reminded her of the young, bewildered father in a situation comedy she'd recently viewed on television. His disciplined, soldier's body bent slightly, mocking the posture of an old man. And he mouthed, "My aching back," for her benefit.

Slowly, his back straightened as he cast her a long, perplexed glance and looked away. He was playing the village idiot, and her children loved it. She laughed, responding to their giggles. Her gaze caught his briefly again. But he dropped his eyes when her two, "golden heads" slipped between them and headed for the toybox. Merrily's eyes followed them, her inner thoughts shifting quickly from wife/lover to mother.

With a deep sigh, she started toward them, determined not to allow her children to open that box and spread toys all over their hotel room. But Garth stopped her, took hold of one slender wrist with a firm grip while hushing her with a forefinger to his mouth.

"Let 'em play," he whispered softly, his eyes beseeching. "I don't mind." Suddenly, she was in his arms.

"Are you sure?" she whispered; her gaze focused briefly on her children once more.

"Positive."

His eyes answered hers with an irresistible pull. She caught her breath achingly as he whispered, "Merrily," into her ear.

When she had given up hope that he'd *ever* kiss her, his lips found hers. She felt wild . . . excited.

Todd shouted from somewhere behind them.

"Don't kiss my mommy!" he yelled.

Blushing hotly, Merrily wrenched away from Garth's arms as if they had just done something ghastly.

CHAPTER 2

MERRILY FROZE, staring down at her two, distraught children for a long moment. Their normally large, gray eyes were huge with jealous rage; their healthy, tanned faces were red and pinched. All action in the room slowed, like an old-fashioned record player that needed a good crank. Merrily felt her whole life flashing before her as if her marriage and her children were slipping away. Garth had tried to warn her that Todd and Suzan were disturbed when he kissed her at the church, but she hadn't listened.

She wanted to reach out to them, hold them and explain about Garth and his new role in their lives. She thought she had done that successfully before Garth arrived. At least she tried. But actually seeing Garth and Merrily holding each other, kissing, was different from merely talking about it. Before it had been a nice story, but now Todd and Suzan were directly involved.

Her imploring blue eyes radiated across the empty space between them. She *had* to make them understand. Yet it was useless. Their little, wounded faces hardened even more.

All at once both children were at Garth's side, jerking at the leg of his brown pants, hitting and kicking him with little, bare feet.

"Stop that!" Merrily scolded and tried to pull

them from him. She managed to capture Suzan, briefly, by the straps of her pink jumper, but Todd escaped her, moving to Garth's other pants leg.

Garth spun around and staggered backwards. Falling on his back across the newly made bed, he swatted the air as if attacked by a swarm of bees. His frantic gesturing must have looked funny to the children because suddenly they were laughing as the battle continued on the bed. All the while Merrily was madly pulling first one and then the other of her children off of his prostrate body. But the process was useless. It was like dropping loose sand in a sieve.

"Tickle tickle," four-year-old Suzan said with a giggle and tried to attack one of Garth's arm pits while five-year-old Todd went for the other one.

Todd's little fingers slipped easily under the dark brown jacket and went right to his target. Garth was certainly uncomfortable but seemed to be trying not to overreact and accidently hurt one of the children. Merrily could also tell that his control was weakening. She had to do something. Fast!

"Don't you like to play tickle tickle, Mr. Butler?" Todd asked.

"No!" Garth exclaimed. "I mean, yes. But if you'll stop, I'll teach you a game that's even better."

Todd looked doubtful. "Promise?" He stopped tickling.

"Promise." Garth glanced helplessly at Merrily and shrugged.

But she only smiled, devilishly, then caught and finally held the children. "Yes, Captain Butler." Merrily positioned the children side by side at the foot of the bed and sank down on the edge of the bed beside them. "Tell us about that new game of yours."

29

Garth rose slowly to a reclining position, resting his vibrant body on one sinewy elbow, and raked his hair. "Yeah. Well, you play the game . . . you play it in bed, see . . . after supper. Yes, that's it . . . when it's time to go to sleep," he explained haltingly, and then he suddenly gained control. "It's a sort of tricky game, though. Everybody has to be real good all evening until bedtime or it doesn't work." The children were spellbound by his apparent skill as a storyteller. "When all the lights are out," he went on, "and everybody's real, real quiet, it happens."

Todd, wide-eyed and enchanted, asked, "What happens, Mr. Butler? I mean, Captain."

"The secret game we're going to play happens."

"But how do you play it?"

"I can't tell you that, Todd, because it's a secret. But your mommy knows, and she'll be only too glad to tell you." Garth smiled mockingly at Merrily, and to the obvious delight of the children, he pretended to hand her an invisible torch. "So what do you say, Mom?"

Merrily faked a sober expression and wet her generous, pink lips. "Well, it's such a secret that I'm not even allowed to tell it all until we're all in bed."

"Is Captain Butler going to sleep in here with us?" Todd asked.

Merrily blushed as Garth answered. "Yes, Todd. I'm going to sleep here from now on."

At that Merrily thought even Garth might blush, but he didn't. He simply shot her a wink and continued talking as if explaining things to small children was something he did every day. Merrily was amazed at his ease with the children and their sudden, positive reaction to him. He'd totally charmed them and appeared charmed by them, but under his

30

hooded, dark gaze, it was hard to tell for certain.

The evening meal in the hotel coffee shop went well. Todd did spill his milk and Suzan rubbed her dirty shoes all over Garth's pants, but the bath turned out to be a reenactment of the great flood. Water was everywhere. By the time the children were finally in their folding cots and had played two rounds of a new, secret version of tickle tickle, Merrily was so tired she forgot why they were there and that technically she was still a bride. The children's attack on her nerves had been brutal.

When later Garth started his own attack in the big bed of a completely different nature, Merrily stiffened and moved slightly away from him. "The children," she whispered, "they'll hear us!"

"How can they hear us, Merrily?" he asked with a tone of amused complacency and reached for her again. "They're sound asleep."

She moved further away, arms crossed determinedly across her breasts. "But they might wake up and see us."

"It's pitch dark in here! How can they see us? I can't see my hand in front of my face." Garth paused. "How about a quick game of tickle tickle?" he asked playfully but in a deep husky voice.

"No!"

"Why not?"

"Because, Garth, I'm their mother . . . Really! I can't just . . . well, you know. I just can't . . . not with them in the room with us. Surely you can see that."

"I can't *see* anything! It's too blasted dark!"

She laughed then, in spite of herself, but he didn't join her. She didn't think he was laughing inwardly either. And suddenly, a silent coldness fell like a thick fog all around them. It seemed to engulf her.

Strangle her. This was supposed to be their honeymoon, and she'd refused him . . . the man she loved. She'd make it up to him, of course. Still she could never make it be this special night again no matter how hard she tried.

"I'm sorry, really I am."

"Yeah? Well I'm sorry, too!"

"It won't always be like this," she continued in a conciliatory tone. "When we get to Germany and into our quarters we'll . . ."

"We're not getting quarters, Merrily." His tone was grim. "I didn't want to tell you, spoil the wedding and all. But I couldn't get quarters. We're on a waiting list, of course. I've managed to find something on the German economy. It's an old house and badly in need of repair, but I think it will do until our name comes up."

"Oh, Garth, I think I like that even better, living among the German people, I mean, instead of at the army base. Don't you?" She paused. "Well, don't you?"

"Oh, I guess so, hon," he mumbled, tossing and turning like a caged animal. Garth punched his pillow. "Look!" The deep, angry tone in his voice tore at her heart. "This bed is getting a little crowded. I think I'll move over to the couch."

"But how can it be too crowded?"

"Just believe me when I say it's too small. Okay?" With a sigh, he rose from the bed taking a pillow with him.

She heard the soft brush of his terry cloth slippers on the carpeted floor, then a loud bang when his foot hit the toybox. There was an expressive cry of pain, a mumbled expletive, and a loud exhalation of breath when, at last, his hard muscled body fell on the couch with a tired thump.

"I love you, Garth," she called across the dark

spaces between them, suppressing a nervous giggle at the total ridiculousness of their present situation. "Really I do."

"Yeah? I love you too," he said, but not convincingly.

The blinding need for him, that had been welling all day, slowly surfaced, building rapidly to a fire of unquenched desire. There could be many lonely nights in the weeks to come. But how would she stand it? The children could separate them again and again. She might find herself saying, "I'm sorry," because of some mischief they got into, a million times or more. She promised herself, there in bed alone, that she'd never lose her sense of humor or her determination to make their marriage work. She was totally committed.

But it was a long time before she fell asleep.

The town of Volksheim was nestled among green hills, and the United States army post where Garth served was situated at the top of the tallest one, the site of an old, World War II German army base. The post was officially titled the 84th Artillery Group Headquarters, and Garth was in charge of group communications. This was a coveted position for a married man because it required fewer field maneuvers than would have been the case had he been in one of the battalions, and assured him more time in town with his family. But by the time they'd settled into the tiny Inn/Hotel, The Volksheimer, after the long ride from Frankfurt, Merrily had already begun to wonder if he wouldn't rather go on maneuvers. At least when they weren't seeing each other, they weren't fighting.

Faced with an entirely new life, the children had been difficult since the wedding and things weren't improving. They'd been terribly frightened when they first arrived in Germany and stuck to Merrily like glue . . . morning, noon, and *especially* at night. At first Garth made a joke of the whole thing. There were no double beds available in the hotel. Germans, it appeared, preferred to sleep alone, at least those that stayed at The Volksheimer with its misleading, Americanized name.

Everybody had his or her own single bed there with boarded sides all around. To Merrily, the beds looked something like a narrow, junior bed in America. The mattresses were of the old German type that divided into three parts in order that they could be aired easily each morning in the wide, shuttered windows. Garth hated them with a passion.

Yet he appeared to love just about everything else about Germany, especially the blonde goddesses that paraded by their hotel that first morning on their way to work at the shops in the village or jobs on the army base. Several seemed to know Garth personally, and Merrily noticed that he'd managed to pick up a lot of the language. She couldn't help wondering if one of the blondes she'd seen had taught him German and what he'd taught her in return.

With almost two weeks of leave time left before he had to report to the army post on the hill, Garth suggested that they spend that time together, alone if possible, and Merrily quickly agreed. The only problem was getting a suitable sitter. She couldn't leave the children with just anybody. She'd been impressed with their round, little, cherry-cheeked landlady at the hotel, however, and finally allowed Frau Languth to keep the children for an hour on their first morning in Volksheim to test how well they got along.

However, that one nervous hour away from the children was torture for Merrily. She really didn't know Frau Languth or any of the other German citizens she'd met at the hotel. How could she have been so lax as to let Garth talk her into leaving Todd and Suzan with a complete stranger? He really didn't care for them or he'd never have suggested such a thing. Anything could happen to two small children in a foreign country unattended. They didn't even have the protection of his name, and he'd made no mention of adopting them. Soon school would be starting for the fall term; she'd have to enter Todd in kindergarten as Todd Knight. If Garth really cared for them, as he pretended, he'd want them to be Todd and Suzan Butler so they could be a real family.

Narrow, cobblestone streets lined with quaint shops flashed by the window on her side of Garth's white Mercedes, but Merrily barely noticed. She was aware, however, of his mounting agitation. The handsome, virile man behind the wheel was beginning to remind her of a raging bull. His nostrils flaring, he suddenly turned and cast her a hot, boldly exciting side-glance. She had to put the children out of her mind and show more of an interest in Garth and his grand tour of the ancient town. Any other time, that look would have sent her, panting, into his arms.

Earlier he'd pointed out the remains of a medieval castle that stood at the edge of Volksheim like a reddish-brown watchman on a high hill opposite the army base, and she'd hardly listened. The children were too important to her to simply block them out of her mind. On the other hand, how could she expect a thirty-four-year-old former bachelor to understand the thoughts and concerns of a parent? That problem wasn't supposed to come up when a couple had been married a mere four days. When she and Mark had been married four days, she remembered, they were still on their honeymoon . . . just the two of them alone in a remote cabin in the Ozark Mountains.

All at once she trembled, wondering longingly what a honeymoon alone with Garth in the mountains would be like. He mentioned taking her to Garmisch or Berchtesgaden for a skiing vacation. She pictured them there together in an alpine ski lodge in front of a roaring fire. She could almost feel his strong arms around her as she cast him a fleeting gaze. It wasn't natural to be young and in love, but never alone. Nor was it right, she reminded herself, to neglect her children in order to achieve that goal. Was there no middle ground? She'd have to find it if there was . . . and quick . . . or risk losing the only man she could ever love.

The scenic drive up the hill to the army base was a blur until, abruptly, Garth stopped the car. He parked and half dragged Merrily into the brown brick building that contained the base snack bar and PX. For a cup of coffee, he said. He wanted her to meet his friends. She was wearing a tight fitting, royal blue knit shirt and matching jeans to Garth's white T shirt and blue denims. Her long, dark hair tumbled loosely about her slender shoulders and blew gently in the soft breeze, giving her an air of femininity that she was not aware of. But Garth seemed acutely appreciative of her obvious charms.

Blue was her color. The soft knit molded the slim, rounded bodice of her shirt and tiny waist to perfection. Still Merrily was dissatisfied with her appearance. The scooped neckline was entirely inappropriate, she thought, for an army post full of gaping soldiers. She hated their naked stares, felt an angry rush of color when two enlisted men in army greens and black boots gave her slender, shapely body a lewd appraisal. Yet Garth didn't seem to notice. He

was so eager to get her inside that he appeared unaware of her growing followers. But, at least, the
raging bull he'd been earlier gentled by the time they
got to the door. He'd even acquired an engaging
smile.

She hadn't expected to see anyone that morning
but Garth and had dressed accordingly. Man had always thought her beautiful. She'd grown accustomed
to it. Still, she felt self-conscious among so many
lonely men far from home. She should have told
Garth to drive her home. But he was enjoying himself. She hated to spoil his first opportunity to introduce her.

"We have exactly twenty-five minutes left." Garth
checked his watch. "Twenty-*four* minutes until you
turn back into a mommy, Merrily, and I'm not about
to waste any of it." The grin widened, and a teasingly knowing glance caressed her eyes and slid
downward to include her frosted lips. "I'd take you
out for a romantic picnic in the bushes somewhere,
but we don't have time." He grinned mischievously.
"Maybe later . . . someplace away from the base if
possible."

He opened the heavy, wooden door. Merrily stepped into the snack bar amidst a sea of hungry stares.
There wasn't another woman in the room except the
old, German lady behind the cashier's counter. All
eyes seemed focused on Merrily. From every direction she sensed them.

She wanted to fall through the floor. Why had he
insisted on bringing her here? Didn't he know how
out of place she felt?

She was only too aware of the words printed in
big white letters across her chest: *MADE IN GER-
MANY.* Even the message chagrined under the glare
of fifty lonely GI's. She could almost see their lips
form the words as they each carefully read it and

smiled.

Take me home! she thought. But she couldn't bring herself to say anything aloud. Garth seemed to delight in showing her off.

The snack bar was no different than dozens of similar ones she'd seen on military posts all over the United States, but Merrily had never felt such a hot burst of embarrassment before in all her life. The room was overflowing with big heavy tables surrounded by cold metal chairs with red plastic seats. Each chair contained a potential Merrily ogler in army fatigues or casual clothes like the ones Garth was wearing. There was a long serving counter at the far end of the room and a hint of a kitchen beyond the swinging, white painted door. Merrily couldn't help wondering if there was an exit door off the kitchen and if she dared seek it.

She glanced up then to find that Garth's pleased expression had vanished on finally noting the looks she was getting. Quickly, he grabbed her arm. "Let's get out of here," he said firmly. He was leading her back toward the door when three especially eager, young lieutenants at a large table toward the back waved at them and smiled. When the men motioned for Merrily and Garth to join them, Garth wanted to refuse. But Merrily didn't want to insult Garth's friends, so she encouraged him to reconsider. Reluctantly, Garth guided her, with a warm hand to her back, in their direction. "Merrily," Garth said with a glimmer of a smile and a trace of pride in his deep, vibrant voice, "I'd like you to meet a couple of the guys." He nodded to all three in general, then turned to the sandy haired man with lazy, gray eyes at the far end of the table. "This is Tom Drake. Over here is Hank Chomas, and this fellow is Smithy." Short, round, and smiling, Smithy blushed slightly as Garth went on. "Joe Smithy

Smith to be exact.''

"Hi," Merrily managed with a forced smile.

To avoid their probing eyes, she carefully scanned the room for something to focus on . . . anything to get her brain off what they were probably thinking. She noticed a poster on the back wall of little children in native, German dress that reminded her of Todd and Suzan, and her mind drifted back again to the children. If only she could know for sure what they were doing at that moment. The minutes dragged. She was frantic by the time they finally started back. And later, she couldn't remember a thing that was said at the table or the name of a single man she'd met.

CHAPTER 3

RELIEF POURED FROM her blue eyes when, at last, Merrily joined her children. They were playing contentedly in the garden behind the hotel with two of Frau Languth's grandchildren and under the Frau's watchful eyes. She'd not seen Todd and Suzan so happy since they left Houston. Garth was quick to pick up Merrily's quelled expression. Before she knew it, he'd asked the kindly Frau if she'd consider keeping the children for the rest of the afternoon so that they could have a picnic up in the hills somewhere.

Frau Languth instantly agreed with her usual, "Dat is good," and insisted on making them a lunch. Merrily was still a little apprehensive about leaving the children again. Yet when she saw how happy they were with their new friends, Kristoff and Annetta, she could hardly refuse.

Garth and Merrily lunched with all four children downstairs in the dining room of the small hotel, then quietly slipped away. Merrily expected another teary scene. The children had cried when she left that morning. But to her surprise, they seemed almost glad that Garth and Merrily were leaving, hardly giving them a backward glance.

The romantic, picnic lunch consisted of the hard German rolls that Merrily was so fond of, cheese, sausage, and a chilled bottle of white wine. Garth brought along his tape player, an assortment of tapes, and his new, Cannon AV-1 camera. They followed the lazy path the Main took for almost an hour, stopped for coffee in a small town and did sightseeing along the way. There were several points of interest including a castle or two. Then they turned south from Wurzburg toward Wertheim where the Main and the Tauber Rivers connected.

Garth had been silent since they left the turn-off at Wurzburg, restlessly lost in his own thoughts. A melting thrill coursed through Merrily, watching his handsome face in profile beside her in the front seat. The straight, almost classical nose was determined and masculine. The firm tightening in his wide, square jaw added an element of power to a chin that was already like granite. His dark, deep-set eyes were edged in long lashes as black as the shock of curly hair that he kept raking unconsciously with one huge hand.

It was scarcely four in the afternoon. Already the warming sun was sinking low behind a grassy hill. Evening shadows played on the planes of his darkly tanned face, accenting high cheekbones and giving his whole body the look of an Indian warrior carved in ebony. Even without his uniform, his tall powerful body dominated any room or situation.

Suddenly, she wanted desperately to be wrapped in those strong, sinewy arms and feel his lips on hers. "Garth," she said in a soft, enticing voice.

"How much longer until we get wherever it is we're going?"

"Not much longer now, hon," he replied without removing his eyes from the winding, two-lane highway. "We'll be there before you know it."

Merrily's hopes slowly faded as she continued to watch him. If only he'd reward her with a word, a glance, or merely a smile. However, she was doomed to disappointment. He kept peering down the road ahead with a hard, purposeful expression . . . as if there was something important he had to do and couldn't give up until he'd done it.

At last she let her head drop lazily to the soft, black leather headrest and closed her eyes. Her mind was a maze of conflicting emotions. She'd thought she knew Garth Butler. He'd been a family friend for years, a favorite of her father's. Merrily was certain, from hearing him talk about his little nephew, that Garth liked children. *But would he ever be a father to Todd and Suzan,* she wondered, as her mind carefully pondered their unique relationship. But only for an instant. Then his deep, vibrant voice assaulted her senses again.

"In fact," he said. "We're here!"

He wheeled to the right, off the main road, and parked in a remote spot by a rippling brook that forked off the blue and silver Main. He made no attempt to emerge from the car. They just sat there, looking at each other for a while as they'd done that day by the lake, their eyes welded together in currents of passion that were practically visible. The communication between them required no words. Each seemed to know what the other was thinking . . . and wanting, and Merrily had never felt closer to him than at that moment.

"Merrily," he said hoarsely but in a deep tone that softened her defenses as well as her heart. "Do you know the story of Jacob and Rachel?"

Her eyes widened in acute surprise. "Like in the Bible?"

"Yes, like in the Bible."

"Not really," she admitted, still spellbound by the dark yearning she saw in his eyes. "I'm a little lacking in that area, I'm afraid."

"Then let me refresh your memory." He slowly moved to her side of the front seat and took her gently in his arms, his eyes never once leaving her beautiful face. "Jacob saw a beautiful, young girl at a well one day and knew instantly that he had to have her. He asked her father for her hand. Her father promised to give her to him when Jacob had worked for him without pay for seven years. Jacob gladly agreed because she was worth waiting for, but when the seven years ended it was not Rachel he married but her older sister Leah. He'd been tricked! A short while later he was allowed to marry Rachel, but he had to work without pay for another seven years." He stopped then and gazed at her even more intently as his face moved closer and closer. "Tell me, my Rachel," he whispered tenderly, his mouth so close she could feel his cooling breath on her cheek. "How many more years must I work for you?"

Startled, Merrily was speechless once again. Why had he called her Rachel, she wondered, as tenderly he whispered her name? Goose flesh attacked her smooth skin on hearing her name spoken with such tender emotion. But her fleeting thoughts raced on. Was he trying to tell her something? Was he saying that she was actually two women, and he wanted only one of them?

"I'm waiting, my Rachel, for your answer," he whispered as his lips brushed hers. He gave her no time to answer, however, but kissed her thoroughly, this time with a demanding passion.

She answered with an eager response to his lingering lips. For a sweet moment all other thoughts vanished. There was only the overwhelming need to feel
his mouth on hers. They sat there holding each other
for a long time. But thoughts of Rachel and the story
kept assaulting her mind. Which sister was she?
Rachel, the wife/lover, or Leah, the woman he didn't
love or want?

Later, when they'd deserted the car in search of a
more private spot, she decided to be Rachel, at least
for a little while. Hand in hand, they climbed to the
top of the hill and gazed out for a silent moment.
Majestic beauty surrounded them: gentle hills, deep,
green valleys, and gingerbread houses with high,
red-roofed peaks. Her nostrils savored the fresh,
cool smells of German summer. Her slender young
body trembled at the promise of kisses to come. It
was the fairyland she'd read about as a child. She
felt blessed to be sharing it for the first time with the
one she loved. Merrily's heart pulsated fiercely, just
knowing Garth was beside her. Her lips softened
with love and a gentle longing.

"You're very beautiful," he faltered, his eyes silently seeking. Her heart pounded in response. Then
his mood took a new turn. "Mary Lee," he tacked
on teasingly.

She turned sharply and lifted her head at a cocky
angle. Brows arched, she pretended anger. "Mary
Lee, did you say?" She paused, then shook her
head. "No, I'm sorry. I don't believe I know anyone
by that name."

Garth's warm chuckle vibrated around her. The
sound of it was almost as exciting as his vibrant
voice. "Remember the first time I called you that?"
His wide grin crinkled the corners of his eyes, eyes
that had softened considerably since they'd been

talking, but with still a dash of mischief. "I remember whether you do or not," he said.

"How could I forget? I could have strangled you," she shot back playfully. "We were within earshot of a cute boy I was trying to impress by the name of Walter Tabson."

"Walter Tabson!" There was a genuineness to his laugh that she found irresistible. "Was that really his name?" She nodded, but his laughter drowned out anything she might have said in reply. "Surely, Mary Lee, you could do better than that."

"That's Merrily."

"Oh, yes. I keep forgetting."

He squeezed her hand, and she felt the heat of it . . . and his probing eyes, so smoldering in their dark depths. "Do you remember what you said to me?" The tenderness she saw in his eyes, his smile, seemed to hold back a flood of stronger emotions. "You said, 'my name's Merrily, as in merrily-we-roll-along.' "

A laugh like a tinkling bell escaped her. "I was a silly kid then, wasn't I?"

His voice and expression were at once intense and serious. "I didn't think so. You were beautiful . . . even then."

His lips trembled with passion. His melting gaze washed her in a barrage of sweet sensations. She felt herself moving naturally into his arms. Sometime earlier he had dropped the carrying case containing the recorder and camera equipment and the heavy, German feather quilt he'd been carrying, and she had put down the lunch basket. Now, as if in a dream, they spread out the quilt on the grassy hilltop together and fell upon it in a fusing embrace laced with sweet, lingering kisses. They made love on the hill with a blinding passion that was glorious.

45

"You're cold," he said, when the sun dipped lower, and he covered them with the smooth, satin quilt.

Like two butterflies wrapped in a single cocoon, they watched the sun die amidst a red gold crescendo of brilliant color. Lying beside Garth and coiled in the memory of their love, Merrily was suddenly glad they'd made love there among the hills with the sky for a backdrop. Stars, like tiny candles, flickered shyly above them. At first there were only three or four, then there were thousands. The lights from the alpine cottages below dotted the countryside, adding to the quiet concert of light.

When night fell, she'd melted even closer to his wide muscled chest. In the cradle of Garth's arms, they made love again there in the moon and starlight. It was past midnight before they got back to the hotel.

Why don't we go into the café and have some chow before we go in, hon?" he asked as, arm in arm, they emerged from the car. He glanced down at her with a squeeze and a tender smile and brushed back a soft, brown curl from her face. "I'm starved!"

"Me, too."

Playfully breaking away from his arms with a coquettish toss of her head, she moved ahead. But with one step he overtook Merrily and kissed her long and hard. Slowly, he released her and opened the trunk of the car, carefully removing their things one by one. She reached for the picnic basket and suddenly realized that they had never eaten their lunch.

"Hey!" she exclaimed. "Why don't we save money and eat our lunch in the room?"

There was a teasing lift to his brow. "Now *that's* an idea!" But his dark eyes told that the hunger she saw there would not be quenched by food. They were both laughing when, together, they hurried inside, up the stairs, and down a dark hall to the door of their suite.

They'd rented two adjoining rooms, but Todd and Suzan had been too frightened, since arriving in Germany, to sleep in their room. It was converted into a sitting room, leaving one big bedroom for Garth, Merrily, and the children.

When, at last, they tiptoed into their room, they found Frau Languth stretched out, fully clothed, in Todd's bed and the children snuggled together in Suzan's. A night light was on, and the old woman was snoring loudly. Merrily had to shake her shoulder several times before finally waking her.

The Frau jerked to wakefulness, muttering something in German with harsh, guttural sounds, then sat up in bed drowsily and rubbed her eyes. "Ah! Herr Butler! Frau Butler," she said haltingly and with a heavy accent. "You are back. Yah? Dat is good."

"Yes," Garth replied, elbowing Merrily knowingly. "Dat was *very* good."

Merrily felt her cheeks glowing with embarrassment in the dimly lit room. His sly reference to their recent encounter flustered her. He paid the kindly Frau and escorted her to the door. When she'd gone and he'd locked the door, he asked, "May I escort you into the sitting room to watch the submarine races? I understand the Main River is famous for them."

Merrily laughed. "Isn't your geography a little backwards, Captain? They only have that on the San Antonio River."

"Are you speaking from experience?" Garth

47

asked in a teasingly bored tone. "Or was that merely a guess?"

"Both."

He raised one brow in obvious jest. "It better not be." He offered her his arm.

Laughing, she hooked her arm under his and gazed up playfully. "Why, Cap'un Butler, I'd be charmed."

At that moment little Todd moaned softly in his sleep. Instantly tuned to the sound of her children's voices, Merrily's arm tensed against Garth's . . . waiting to see what the child would do. Slowly, Todd opened his eyes and rubbed them, then sat up in bed.

Turning to Merrily who was still standing apprehensively in the doorway beside Garth, Todd said, "Mommy, can I have a glass of water?"

Merrily glanced briefly at Garth, hoping for understanding, then shot forward toward the child's bed. Bending over him with obvious tenderness, she stroked his tossled, gold curls, and spoke with gentle assurance. "Of course you can have some water, sweetie. I'll go get it right away. But first, wouldn't you be more comfortable in your own bed?"

The child didn't answer but allowed her to move him to the other bed and cover him with a light blanket. Patting the boy's head, she glanced back at Garth . . . a tall shadow in the doorway. "I'm sorry." She paused. "I'm beginning to sound like a broken record, aren't I? But this can't be helped. I'll be along in a little while, if you don't mind waiting."

"I'm used to waiting for you, Merrily. I've never minded waiting for what I want." He hesitated then, as if to emphasize his next statement. "But my patience does have its limits."

The jovial good humor and understanding he'd displayed that night after their evening under the stars quickly faded. During the next three weeks, the story about Rachel and his warning "that his patience had limits" haunted her. It was not until a few days before moving day that the children finally agreed to sleep in their own room. By then a wall of silence separated Merrily and Garth. Even the joy they shared in each other's arms didn't remove its constant presence. Merrily was determined, however, to find some way to break it down no matter how long it took. Something was lacking in their marriage, but she had not a hint as to what it might be.

Her life as the wife of an army officer had also taken shape in those long weeks before they moved into their rented, German house. She'd attended several "get acquainted" teas at the officers club on the base and had been delightfully enchanted with the wife of the commanding officer, Lilly Arkin.

Merrily had also made a friend of her own age, Shelly Trenton, and an enemy, Dell Phillips. Everyone else she'd met was just a blur of faces and a jumble of names. Only those names stood out in her mind but for entirely different reasons.

On the day she and Garth moved into the rented cottage across the river from the hotel, Merrily met the teenaged wife of an enlisted man. The two rented a small apartment in their landlord's house next door. Her name was Polly Stardard. Though Merrily hadn't met her husband Bob, she liked Polly immediately.

There was a certain helpless vivaciousness radiating from her big, amber eyes, that struck a harmonic chord in Merrily. She found herself wanting to mother the girl, take Polly under her wing right away, and Polly appeared only too willing.

The house at 12 Wasser Strasse was at least two

hundred years old, Garth estimated, a two-story brown brick affair with a high-pitched red roof, its own cellar, and a coal bin. Merrily was enchanted with its ample size and charm. The furnace had been converted to gas years before. The coal bin was still equipped with a scattering of both soft and hard coal and a few logs slashed to fit the tiny door of the old, black furnace. She envisioned finding a hidden treasure there to the delight of the children. Two big bedrooms and a bath filled the upstairs. An entry, a living room, and dining room/kitchen made up the downstairs area. In the master bedroom an antique, walnut armoire closeted some of Merrily's clothes, Garth's suits and pants, and his dashing army captain's dress uniform complete with brass buttons, medals, and gold braid.

Merrily, an antique collector, was thrilled when she first saw the armoire and was amazed when she read *1760* printed in inlaid wood on the front. Their house contained a clothes cupboard that was built before America was even a nation! Yet to the people of Volksheim, old was the medieval castle on the outskirts of town.

Garth had insisted that they hire a capable maid/sitter even before they moved to the cottage from the downtown hotel, and Merrily agreed. The children were becoming more and more a gulf between them. She was willing to do anything to reduce that gulf. He knew of a German girl, Helga Gerber, who was the younger sister of the girl his friend, Lt. Tom Blake, took out. Helga sounded like a dream come true. She'd accepted the salary Garth suggested through Tom without a thought and was willing to "live in" if they wanted her full-time.

Still Merrily balked at that idea. The two upstairs bedrooms were separated only by the connecting bath. She was not about to have a young girl under foot day and night. Merrily finally agreed to Garth's suggestion that they put an extra, single bed in the children's room so that Helga could stay overnight when they really wanted her. That was before Merrily met Helga.

Far from the timid wallflower she'd expected, Helga was smashing to look at despite her lack of makeup. The tall, willowy girl's pink-cheeked face, golden hair, and green, flashing eyes, radiated health and vitality. With her face and figure, Merrily was sure that Helga would be a wash-out as a sitter/maid, but even there Helga shined. She filled every duty with the skill of a pro. Still, Merrily neither liked or trusted the girl. She was a little too friendly with Garth for Merrily's taste. Once when Helga didn't know she was watching, Merrily caught her gazing at Garth as if he was Prince Charming in the flesh. At eighteen, Helga was almost nine years younger than Merrily, but seemed not lacking in experience.

Merrily had hoped to put off having Helga at the cottage as long as possible, but on the night they moved in there was an important reception at the Officers Club on the post. Helga was expected to sit with the children at least until they returned.

Helga arrived early and took the children directly upstairs to their room to play, leaving Merrily blissfully free to take a lazy bath and cream shampoo her hair. She was combing her hair, dressed only in a half slip, bra, and panties, when Garth came home. His brisk footfalls on the hardwood stairs and the smell of pipe tobacco were unmistakable. Knowing her allergic reaction to tobacco smoke, he never smoked in her presence, but his clothes were often tinged with the scent of it.

She looked up from her stool in front of the makeshift dressing table and smiled as he came in

51

the bedroom door. He smiled back at her, and her heart started the usual jumping.

"*Guten Tag*, lovely lady," he said warmly. "Are you ready to dazzle the seventh army at the wing-ding tonight?"

"Almost."

Pale blue walls and frothy white curtains contrasted the dark brilliance of his gaze. He was still in his uniform, which made him look taller than his six feet three inches. She'd never noticed how close he came to brushing the top of the doorway. His broad, muscled shoulders had always been something to dream about. She felt a blinding urge to be crushed against his wall-like body. Yet her stubborn self-control wouldn't allow her to speak her feelings. A major's daughter didn't—ever! And he'd been so cold lately.

"I just have to slip on my dress."

An embarrassing silence engulfed Merrily as she tried hard to control the rosy color that had touched her skin with an ethereal glow. The sensuous grin that played on his lips and the gleam in his eyes told her exactly what he was thinking, and that he'd guessed her thoughts, too. "Don't get dressed on my account," he teased.

"Now Garth, don't get any ideas. You know perfectly well that we can't be late for this thing tonight . . . and there's a good chance we will be if you don't jump right in the tub."

"That's an idea!" His eyes brightened. "Care to join me?" He reached for her as the shrill, piercing ring of the telephone cut mercilessly into their world.

Merrily tensed in his arms. He wanted to kiss her, and she wanted him to. But she couldn't ignore the phone. The phone rang again, bombarding their ears with its sound. Neither of them moved or attempted to answer it. Again, it sounded . . . and again. Merrily's heart pounded. She couldn't just let it ring on and on. Reluctantly, she accepted the results of her moral upbringing. She sighed deeply and picked up the receiver.

CHAPTER 4

"CAPTAIN BUTLER'S QUARTERS, Mrs. Butler speaking," she managed in her best army-wife voice.

"Well, hello, Mrs. Butler speaking," Tom said with a playful laugh. "This is Tom Drake. Remember me? We met at the snack bar up on the hill with Garth."

Merrily's heart fell, annoyed. Their embrace had been hindered for nothing more important than a phone call from Tom Drake, the playboy soldier. It would be difficult not to reveal her displeasure in her voice.

"Oh, yes, Lieutenant Drake," she said stiffly. "How nice to hear from you again. Are you calling for my husband?"

"Not necessarily," he paused. "I'm hoping to engage you two in a little mischief after the torture session at the O Club tonight."

Merrily froze. Garth had told her all about Tom, and she didn't like what she'd heard. Any suggestion Tom made was sure to displease her.

"Inga and I know of a little place down in the town that serves the best rum steak in the entire world," Tom explained. "Are you game?"

"Well, I really don't know. If you'll hold on a minute, I'll ask Garth." Covering the mouthpiece, she turned with a frown to Garth, who was seated on the side of the bed beside her, and shook her head in an obvious *no*. "It's Tom and he wants us to go out with him and Inga for rum steak after the reception." She was begging him to refuse with her expressive, blue eyes. Pleading. If there was anything she didn't want, it was to spend an evening with Helga's sister. If she could believe Garth, Inga looked something like a German movie star only better. A "blonde bombshell" were his exact words. But it wasn't that. She just wanted to be alone with Garth.

But he seemed to want to go out with them. He got that "be mature, Merrily" look in his eyes and lifted his strong chin condescendingly. "I think it would be good for both of us to go out for a little while. We can't be parents *all* the time."

The reference to parents cut to the core. She knew what he was really implying, that she was a full-time mother and no wife at all. She knew they needed to talk about their relationship, yet she never seemed to find the right moment to bring the subject to his attention. There was always something more urgent to discuss. With a sigh, she had to admit that it often had to do with *her* children.

"Well, what do you say, hon?" he asked after a long silence. "Shall we act like newlyweds tonight? Or an old, married couple?" His face brightened encouragingly. "Come on! It might be fun."

"Oh, all right." Blandly, she handed the phone to Garth.

He put the receiver to his ear and seemed to take

55

on an entirely different personality. He was the charming, debonair, army captain again, the man she'd found so fascinating before they married. "Tom Drake, you old warhorse," he said in that deep, resonant voice that drove her wild. "Have you been trying to go after my beautiful wife?" Tom must have said something funny because Garth laughed and said, "Ah ha! So I've caught you then in the act! Now what's this I hear about some savage attack on rum steak you've been planning? . . . Sounds good . . . . Oh, I see. Inga has to work late so you'll pick her up later. Okay, fine. How soon after the wake at the O Club do you think we can safely slip away? . . . All right then. It's a deal. See you there, Tom."

I don't like rum steak, Merrily thought as she took the receiver from him and hung up the phone. But she knew that was the least of her problems.

The officers club on the hill was situated at the remote north end of the army post. The drive up from the valley in their white Mercedes Benz was usually a joy, even in the semi-darkness of an August evening. The well-tended flowers that skirted the open fields along the way were not visible, and the tall trees that lined the paved road were mere shadows. *Shadows,* she thought, recalling Garth's dark mood when they left the house. The muscles in Merrily's stomach balled, remembering Garth's face when she thoughtlessly compared his action to Mark; the comparison was definitely not in Garth's favor. An apology hadn't helped. If that wasn't enough, they were almost late for the party, and it was her fault. Her hair and makeup had never taken longer.

Casually she glanced out at the red-roofed gingerbread houses that dotted the countryside below, pretending not to care that he was still angry. But she wasn't thinking about landscapes as they snaked the alpine road to the top of the hill. It would be a difficult evening at best.

Many of the original, red brick buildings constructed for the German army were still standing. The Americans, who currently occupied the base, had been perceptive enough to continue with the same architectural style. Group Headquarters had a unique, Old-World charm. Merrily never felt completely transported back to the states even when she shopped in the very American PX and commissary. It was too German in tone and style. Yet all she could think of, as they turned off the main road toward the club, was how unhappy she was and how she wished she was home with her family and that Garth wasn't so angry.

She was wrong to compare Garth to Mark. Still, Mark had been very important to her. It was hard to block out three years of her life.

Inside, the officers' club was like a big, white plaster barn dotted with colorful murals. The warmth of the room, the smiling faces, only added to the pain of seeing Garth's dark expression. Wainscoting covered every wall topped with ornately carved molding, an example of the best in German craftsmanship. The huge beams that lined the white ceiling were also carved and matched beautifully with the gingerbread chairs and heavy, oak tables. At any other time Merrily, with her love of old, quaint objects, would have been enchanted.

An attractive mural, complete with green hearts and a tangle of yellow and red flowers, hung dramatically over the huge oak bar and serving table at the far end of the room. Most of the crowd had already gravitated to that area. She noticed her new friend Shelly Trenton and her husband as she and Garth went through the motions of going through the stuffy, receiving line.

Merrily had had many black friends. But Shelly and her husband Mike were her first black *best* friends. They were what Merrily called solid, family types with three young children and a very large dog.

Shelly was tall and slender. Her creamy skin was not much darker than Merrily's. Long black hair curved seductively across one side of her lovely, fine-boned face. Mike was somewhat darker but equally attractive. He was almost as tall as Garth, and even more muscular.

Garth and Mike had been good friends when they were stationed together at Fort Carson, Colorado, but when Garth made captain, Mike cooled. It wasn't that Mike wasn't happy about Garth's success. It was simply that he resented West Pointers. They seemed to make rank a little too fast for their own good in Mike's estimation. West Point was never a security blanket for Garth, but Mike seemed threatened by it.

Garth's deep, icy voice tore suddenly into her thoughts. "You have your friends and I have mine," his cold gaze stung painfully. "I suggest we join them."

Heartsick, she drifted toward Shelly while Garth headed directly for Tom Drake and several other single officers. Tom wouldn't be picking up Inga until nine. Until then, he was available, too available to Merrily's way of thinking. Tom was probably a good friend to have if you were single and looking for action, but he was a disaster zone for a married man who wanted to stay married. What Merrily hadn't decided yet was whether or not the latter applied to Garth. Did he want to stay married for always as she did? She'd stopped trembling when she reached Shelly, standing alone and facing the massive, red brick fireplace. "Hi, Shell."

Shelly turned with a smile that lighted her whole face. "Hi. I was hoping you'd be here."

"Did I have a choice?"

"Not really, I guess."

Shelly Trenton was smashing in a simple, red jersey sheath under a whispy, see-through caftan. Her outfit was a dead ringer for one in Merrily's closet that she'd considered wearing that night. Thankfully, Merrily had chosen the blue crepe, her going away dress. It molded her slender form to perfection. More important, nobody was wearing one exactly like it.

Most of Merrily's clothes were being shipped from Houston. She'd only been allowed to bring a few basics on the plane. Now her red caftan was out. But did it matter what she wore? Garth never noticed.

"I love your outfit, Shelly." Merrily's smile was a tribute to her ability as an actress. She felt like crying.

"I love yours, too."

They were standing a little away from the crowd but with an excellent view of everyone there. Merrily found herself searching the room for Garth in a sea of dress uniforms as she went on talking. "In fact, I like your outfit so much that I have one at home exactly like it." Unable to find Garth in the crowd, she turned her attention back to Shelly. "You've got excellent taste, I might add."

"You're kidding about having a dress like this. Aren't you?"

"No such luck." Merrily feigned an air of brightness. "Why does my only friend in all of Germany have to like exactly what I like?"

Shelly laughed. "I have the same problem. So

what shall we do? Wear it on alternate days? I get Saturdays!"

"That only leaves me with Friday and Sunday. Can you imagine me wearing something so 'after-fiveish' when I drop the kids off at Sunday school at the base on Sunday morning?"

"I can't imagine you anywhere near a church on Sunday morning."

"If you're getting ready to start another of your famous 'you need Jesus' routines, you can can it, Shell." Merrily gave a helpless sigh. "I've just about had it tonight." She nodded toward the group of single men. "Clothes and a discussion of fashion are safer, don't you think?"

"I think you need to go to church *with* the kids, not drop them off. But I wouldn't advise wearing that dress you're wearing now. It's a little . . . after-fiveish, too. Don't you think?"

"I will wear it though," Merrily reflected. "It has a matching jacket, and I actually wore it after our wedding reception."

"I keep forgetting that you're a bride." Shelly's dark eyes shifted automatically to Garth and Tom across the room.

"So does my husband, I'm afraid."

Though no words were spoken, knowing looks were instantly exchanged. Merrily found herself scanning the room for Dell Phillips, the lieutenant colonel's wife. Lieutenant Colonel Phil Phillips was at least twenty years older than his beautiful wife.

Dell had hinted, at their first meeting, that she and Garth had had something going before he suddenly left Germany and flew to Houston to get married.

"We're old friends," she'd said, "and *very* close." That was all she'd said. Yet the way she said it left no doubt.

She wouldn't have given Dell's threat another

thought if her marriage were better, but things being as they were, she had to be especially careful. Dell was obviously willing and Garth was vulnerable. Quivering, Merrily bit her lip, trying to erase the thought of them together.

As Merrily stood there watching Dell bubble in the receiving line, Dell suddenly deserted it. Slinking all the way across the room, Dell joined Garth. She was wearing a silver lamé dress that was backless and practically frontless. Merrily stiffened noticeably as her heart pulled inward . . . into a hard knot.

"Are you okay?" Shelly asked, inclining her dark head in the direction of Dell and Garth with narrowed, black eyes.

"I guess so." But she was lying. She was far from okay, and she was sure her face showed it. Her racing heart was already in knots.

"You don't need that, honey," Shelly continued, taking hold of one shoulder and attempting to point Merrily in the direction of the serving table. "What you need is something to eat. Okay?"

"Okay."

Merrily stiffened, fighting back tears, as Dell planted a kiss on her husband's available lips. She needed to ignore them or do something about the situation. She hated herself because she could do neither. At that moment she was rooted to the hardwood floor: her blue gaze fastened to the shattering scene before her.

Merrily shuddered as Dell's jewelled arms tightened around Garth's neck, her palms pressed possessively against the back of his head. Garth's arms dropped loosely to his sides, she noticed, as if he were not a full partner in the long, lingering kiss. Still Merrily felt sick all the way to her bones. She never experienced such feelings of violence toward another woman in her life. Another woman had

61

kissed Mark at a party once, but she saw it as merely an innocent gesture.

It wasn't Garth's fault, Merrily reminded herself. Dell had sought him out, not the other way around. Why did she suddenly have the cowardly desire to run away and hide in the rest room?

When she'd kissed Garth thoroughly, Dell waved with a superficial smile and called to Merrily in a piercing voice from across the room. Practically everybody turned in order to watch Merrily's reaction. It took every bit of willpower she had to shrug off-handedly and smile back at Dell as if they were best friends.

She felt dead inside. She didn't notice the tall form moving steadily toward her as she turned and followed Shelly to the refreshment table.

All at once she felt a warm hand touch her shoulder. She looked up wide-eyes into the hazel gaze of Steve Allison, a boy she'd dated in high school in San Antonio when her father was stationed at Fort Sam Houston. "Steve Allison!" she exclaimed excitedly. "What in the world are you doing so far away from the Lone Star State of Texas?"

"Serving my country bravely, I hope." He laughed charmingly in that special way that Texans laugh even when dressed in the uniform of an army lieutenant and in a foreign country. "What else?" he asked, braking his laugh to a generous smile. "But what are you doing here, Merrily? Is your father stationed somewhere in Germany?"

"No, my father's retired and I'm . . ."

"The best looking woman here," he finished for her. "That's what you were going to say, wasn't it?"

"I'm afraid not." She laughed nervously as she glanced up into his hazel eyes again and saw a startlingly tender look in his handsome face that was quite unexpected. Taken aback, she forgot completely what she'd meant to say.

"Care to dance?" Steve asked in a voice too intimate to be coming from the mouth of merely an old, high school classmate.

Merrily started to refuse. Then Garth and Dell whirled by in what appeared to be a world of their own. She heard herself say, "I'd be delighted."

Steve's sandy-blond hair and broad shoulders brought back sweet memories of another life: of carefree days and football nights, bonfires and boat rides down the San Antonio River. She needed something cheerful to brighten her thoughts, and pleasant memories of Steve was the perfect medicine. She'd had a secret crush on Steve Allison for months before he finally asked her for that all important first date to the senior prom. However, the tender whirlwind of first love was soon quieted. Her father's orders to report to Fort Lewis, Washington, arrived the morning after Steve asked her to be his girl forever. The family moved right after high school graduation.

Merrily and Steve wrote back and forth for a while, of course, but it was never the same. He had been a joyous page in her scrapbook of pleasant memories. It felt good to remember them again as they danced together after so long. It was like a clean blanket of snow after the dirty feeling she'd had on seeing Garth and Dell kissing.

Her thoughts were interrupted when Steve said, "Mer, remember the night I asked you to be my girl?"

"Yes," she managed softly.

"Well," he continued in a breathy, emotional voice. "I still feel the same way I did then. I know it sounds crazy after all these years. But I knew for sure the moment I noticed you tonight. It was like we'd never been apart."

Suddenly the implications of what he was saying snapped her back to reality. She'd used him terribly by not telling him at once that she and Garth were married. To do so now, after what he'd just said, would be needlessly cruel. She had to think of some way to lessen the blow. Panic invaded her. What could she say now?

"I'll always feel something for you, Steve," she said shakily, yet gently. "You were my first love, you know. Nobody ever forgets that. You're a part of my past that I'll always remember, and after we finish dancing, I want to introduce you to my husband . . . or maybe you know him," she looked up at him questioningly, "Captain Garth Butler."

"Butler?" he said scathingly and with a stunned expression. "Oh, sure." He shrugged nervously and tried to smile. "I know him. I've only met a few of my fellow officers, so far, but I do know Captain Butler, of course. He's in communications."

"Yes. But I'm not entirely sure what he does. We've only been married a few weeks. My first husband, Mark Knight, was killed in an auto crash in Houston after we'd been married just three years. My two children are Mark's."

"You have children?"

Merrily laughed, feeling more relaxed. "I most certainly do. Todd is five and Suzan is four, and they are the most beautiful children in the world."

"They'd have to be with you as their mother."

Merrily dropped her eyes. The smile slowly faded. She needed a friend, and she'd hoped her revelation about Garth would put her friendship with Steve back on the right track. It hadn't worked. He was still looking at her as if they were back in high school, and she was still *his* girl.

She had no idea how to handle the situation, though the general problem was nothing new. Some of Mark's friends at work had also made passes at Merrily at company parties. She'd always left feeling slightly embarrassed, wondering if she'd somehow led them on.

To Merrily, there was a thin line between male-female friendships and extramarital flirting. She'd always been careful never to cross that line. Some of the men and women she'd known, however, had crossed over without a backward glance. It had become almost commonplace among some people she knew. In Merrily's estimation, Dellanor Phillips crossed that line the moment she clapped her eyes on Garth from across the room. It was obvious that Dell wanted one thing, and it had nothing to do with friendship.

The music stopped. Steve followed Merrily in the direction of Garth and Dell Phillips. Merrily felt that she had to bring Steve to her husband to satisfy her personal need to keep things light. Steve had to understand that their friendship was going nowhere. At least, she *hoped* he would take the hint. Her throat tightened as she opened her mouth to speak.

"Garth," Merrily said loudly, causing both Garth and Dell to turn toward them and stare. Her heart was racing under Dell's cold appraisal. "I believe you know Steve Allison." She faltered, "and this is Dellanor Phillips, Steve. She's the wife of Lieutenant Colonel Phillips."

"I'm honored to meet you, Mrs. Phillips."

"Dell."

"Dell." Steve smiled after a slight hesitation. "And I'm glad to see you tonight, Sir," he said to Garth in a formal tone.

Garth nodded stiffly. "Lieutenant." His piercing, black eyes raked Steve coldly, and there was a questioning lift to his strong chin.

Dell was looking at Steve, too, but her expression was anything but cold.

"How long have you known my wife?" Garth asked Steve finally, temporarily ignoring Merrily.

"We went to high school in San Antonio together," Steve explained, rather calmly considering the looks he was getting from Garth. "I had no idea she was living in Germany until I saw her here tonight."

"Have you met many people since you arrived here, Lieutenant Allison?" Dell put in with a toothy grin to Steve, then Garth.

Merrily was amazed at Dell's ability to flirt with two men simultaneously. It was almost a talent with the red-haired siren. But more than that, she was puzzled by Garth's reaction to Steve's presence. Perhaps he met Steve years ago, during his visit when they lived in San Antonio, and just now remembered him.

"I've not met many people, I'm afraid," Steve replied after a long pause. "I've only been here a short time." Steve glanced at Garth and continued. "My superiors keep me pretty busy."

"We never met in San Antonio, did we Lieutenant?" Garth said as if answering Merrily's thoughts.

"No, Sir, I don't believe we did. I was . . . ."

"Don't tell me you're that new man Garth's been telling us about!" Dell exclaimed with a dramatic flourish, cutting into Steve's words.

Steve blushed and slowly nodded. "I'm afraid so."

"He says you're a whiz," Dell went on, "a regular quiz kid." Garth continued to glare at Steve, and Steve appeared slightly uncomfortable. Still Dell chattered on. "A group of us are going for rum steak at a little place downtown. Now, say you'll go

Lieutenant. Because I just won't take no for an answer." Steve looked doubtful. "Garth and Merrily are going, of course," Dell said, "and that will give you and Merrily a chance to have a real visit. I'm sure you two have a *lot* of catching up to do."

"In that case." Steve smiled with a teasing glance to Merrily. "You can count me in."

"Well, I hate to break up what sounds like such a nice evening," Garth related with a slight edge to his deep voice. "But I'm not feeling my best tonight, and I promised Merrily an early evening. So I guess we won't be joining you."

Startled, Merrily gazed up at Garth. He wasn't sick; he was telling her something. Garth's tender glance surged through her. She had to force herself to remain calm and listen to what the others were saying.

"What a shame," Dell said coyly. "We'll certainly miss you; won't we Steve? I mean Lieutenant."

"We most certainly will." Steve looked longingly at Merrily.

"Would you mind giving Tom our regrets, Dell?" Garth shot Merrily a devouring look that sent her heart spinning again. "He's gone to pick up Inga, I believe."

"I'd be glad to deliver your message," Dell said, giving Garth "equal time" in the flirting department. "Of course."

"Then if you'll excuse us." Garth nodded first to Dell and then to Steve. "I'd like to dance with my wife." His deep voice had a rich resonance loaded with tenderness. He gazed hungrily at Merrily. "If she'll have me."

Merrily drifted dreamily into his arms. Together, they moved to the soft, slow beat of the instrumental music that wafted from the taped sound system. Garth had always been a satisfactory dancer. At that

67

moment he seemed to almost breathe the lazy rhythms . . . carrying Merrily with him, away from all thought of anyone else.

"I'm sorry, sweetheart, about that kiss," he whispered tenderly in her ear. "But it wasn't my fault and neither was the dance. She kissed me just like she asked me to dance, and that kiss was way out of line . . . in front of all these people, too." He was silent for a moment as waves of longing radiated from his eyes to hers. "I don't know why I've been such a cad tonight. You should have given me a good swift kick in the pants." He hesitated, and squeezed her hand. "Dell invited herself to go for rum steak, too. Nobody asked her."

"I know," Merrily said softly. "It wasn't your fault. I saw the whole thing."

"Well, I was a little worried, knowing how things have been lately between us. Then when I saw you talking and then dancing with your high school sweetheart, I felt like punching the guy in the nose." He peered questioningly at her for a moment. "Did you know he was here in Germany, Merrily?"

"No, but I'm flattered that you felt like hitting him and awfully glad you didn't." She gazed at him lovingly. "Especially when it brought such . . . ardent results."

They exchanged smiles and he held her a little tighter.

"I gathered that you know Steve on the base," she tacked on.

"Oh, yes. I thought I told you that. He's in my outfit." He squeezed her hand again. "So what are we doing here anyway?" he asked.

His tone was deep and throaty. Lowering his head, he planted a kiss on her neck just below her ear. "Let's go home?" he whispered. "How about it?"

She didn't have to answer. Her eyes did it for her. She got her purse. They were already at the door when Tom and the blonde bombshell arrived.

Inga's white dress was of a thin, almost transparent material that outlined her every curve. She was tall and large boned but not at all fat. Merrily thought Inga would have been as comfortable behind a plow as flashed on a movie screen.

Inga hung onto Tom's every word while he and Garth talked. It didn't stop her from glancing invitingly at Garth now and then, however. Merrily wondered if all women on army posts flirted with every man they saw or if they just flirted with *her* husband. Growing up, she'd been too naive to notice such things. She'd been well aware of the problem since arriving in Volksheim though. According to Shelly, some of the army wives could hardly wait until their husbands went on field maneuvers so they could hit the singles bars and clubs.

While all Inga's beguiling signals were flashing loud and clear in Garth's direction, Garth was sincerely trying to get out of going for rum steak. But his efforts were pointless. Tom informed them, on the sly as he put it, that the get together was actually a surprise wedding party for the two of them; they simply *had* to attend.

Suddenly they were all heading for the parking area, then speeding down the hill, caravan style, toward the café behind Tom's red Buick with Steve Allison and a host of others trailing along behind. The best little rum steak place in the entire world turned out to be a place called The Löwin in the oldest part of town.

The Löwin was a red brick building and rather plain on the outside. Inside, the small restaurant was steeped in Old-World charm. An aura of quaint coziness and pleasant, cooking smells invaded Merrily's senses the moment she stepped in the door. Briefly, she forgot all her reasons for not wanting to be there. She found herself smiling broadly at Garth and her host, Tom Drake, in excited anticipation.

Like the officer's club on the base, wainscoting covered the lower half of every wall. The hand-carved molding that lined the top of it was, however, of a finer, more intricate design. Merrily couldn't help running her fingers across a smooth, delicately carved flower before following a round little waiter in short leather pants to the long table next to the dance floor.

A display of beer steins, in various colors and sizes, decorated a large, pine display case that served as a room divider separating the kitchen from the dining area. A small German band, in Lederhosen over long-sleeved white shirts, stood in readiness to begin the evening's entertainment.

Garth was hastily seated between Dell and the blonde bombshell while Merrily shared honors with Tom and Steve Allison. Garth had not seemed in the least displeased with *his* seating arrangement. He glared broodingly across the table at Merrily, however, when he saw Steve, in the chair beside her, giving her his complete attention.

Merrily ordered wiener schnitzel and gave a fair impression of eating it. Her eyes and her thoughts were clearly on her husband's face and commanding form. His handsomeness was always startling. She was almost glad she'd not been seated beside him. She had a better view of his bronzed face in his dress uniform.

He knew she'd been watching him. A hint of a dimple punctuated Garth's brief smile. Then Steve leaned his head toward Merrily and a frown dashed away Garth's smile. It didn't return until the huge, beautifully decorated wedding cake was brought in, and Garth and Merrily were asked to cut it.

Dancing followed the feasting. Steve was quick to partner Merrily in the first dance, drawing her close as a German polka blared from the small, raised bandstand that centered the back wall. The wooden dance floor was tiny, and Merrily was chagrined to find that nobody else felt like dancing. She and Steve were the center of attraction.

All the old dance steps they'd perfected during their high school years came back to her along with the memories. Her shapely body was finely attuned to Steve's every move, blooming under his firm lead with an ease and grace she'd forgotten she possessed. Her blue eyes flashed as he whirled her around, her cheeks glowing with excitement. Merrily's high-heeled white sandals clicked softly as they glided, then floated across the polished, wood floor. The matching rhinestone combs that held back her long, brown hair, sparkled with a hundred lights. Yet even the rhinestone combs dulled in contrast to the brilliance of her smile. She heard herself laugh time and time again. She was almost sorry when the dance ended and Steve escorted her back to the table and Garth's raging glare.

Garth had always hated showy demonstrations, like the one she and Steve had just performed. He'd never been one to dance at all unless the floor was uncomfortably crowded. Suddenly he pulled Merrily out for the next dance, a slow song, and again, nobody joined them. She could feel his breath against her cheek, hear his breathing. He was holding her much too close for polite society. She felt a rush of embarrassment mixed with the poignant smell of tobacco.

After the first few steps he stopped. They just stood there holding each other in front of all their

71

friends and a lot of laughing Germans. Even the band members, in short leather pants, were watching them. Garth hardly ever drank. But he'd had more than one beer that night. She could smell it. What was happening to him? What was happening to *them*? Their marriage. He'd never been like this before—ever.

Garth was the king of the lions showing all the cubs exactly where their boundaries were. "You're mine," he whispered in her ear. His lips moved demandingly on hers. When she tried to pull away, their audience laughed even more.

She deeply resented being put on exhibition. Her hot, rosy cheeks showed it. Yet Garth appeared determined to make his point. She was his property, in case Steve hadn't gotten the message earlier. The kiss went on and on.

"That away!" Tom jeered disgustingly from the sidelines. "Go for it!"

Garth slowly released her and glanced back at Tom. "That's exactly what I'm planning to do." Garth's voice was loud enough for everyone to hear. "So if you'll all excuse us, I'll take my little mama home."

He's drunk! she thought venomously. Otherwise, he'd never have said that. She felt like a fool. Angrily, she turned away from him.

The crowd roared with applause exactly like football fans did back in Texas when the Dallas Cowboys scored. If she could have disappeared into the woodwork, she would have. At that moment she had a blinding urge to claw Garth Butler's handsome face with both hands; her whole face clearly showed it. She was amazed at her own self-control in not acting upon her impulses.

"Get your purse, honey," Garth commanded, taking her arm and guiding her back to the table. "I'll meet you at the door.''

How could he humiliate her in this unspeakable way? And after he put Dell down for kissing him, too. Could he possibly do such a thing if he really cared? *Little Mama, indeed!* Dell and the blonde bombshell probably enjoyed every second of her ordeal.

"I'm sorry, hon," Garth said when she'd gotten her purse and they were heading for the car. "I guess I had a little too much to drink tonight. You and that German beer kind of went to my head."

"How flattering!" Stopping there in the parking lot, a hand on each hip, she glared at Garth indignantly. "You mentioned me before the beer! I can't believe you'd put me above a stein of beer."

"I didn't mean anything by that, Merrily. You looked so beautiful and . . . "

"What did you mean making a spectacle of me in front of all those people?" Her lips were drawn tightly across grinding, white teeth. "I'll never be able to face *any* of them again! Ever!"

"Sure you will, honey." Garth reached for her, then held her against his chest like he'd done on the dance floor. "They know we're newly married. They were probably expecting something like this."

"The show must go on! Is that it?" she blared, turning her head to the side and trying to pull away from him. "I thought you hated vain displays. And I never dreamed you'd ever try to embarrass me in public."

"It was all in fun, honey. I never meant to embarrass you. But nevertheless, I'm sorry."

His deep voice touched her with a caress of gentle reassurance. But Merrily was too enraged to stop her now pointless assault. It was like a rising river that couldn't be averted.

"Sorry, you say!" Her face, like her voice, blazed

with pent up emotions. Her blue eyes narrowed angrily, lashing through his tender smile. "Sorry for who, Garth? . . . Dell or the blonde bombshell?"

"Neither." His face darkened with sudden fury as he abruptly released her. "I was thinking of you, Merrily." A trace of mockery colored the deep, steady voice. "But I'm sure you would have enjoyed making a display with Mar . . . with that man whose name I dare not reveal." He gazed at her narrowly. "Wouldn't you, my dear?"

"Maybe I would!" she shot back hotly.

Briefly, she saw once more that same pained expression she first saw on their wedding night, and seeing it was like a deep stab to her heart. She'd hurt him again. She wanted to say something, make amends. But again, no words surfaced. She watched, as if in limbo, as he stiffly led her to the car with frightening indifference.

She loved him. There was no doubt. And she sensed that he loved her, too, in his way. Yet something was lacking in their marriage, something that had nothing to do with Garth's senseless jealousy of either Steve or Mark. It even went beyond her jealous feelings toward Dell, Inga, and that child, Helga. It was as if the glue designed to bind them together forever was missing or hidden somehow. And she had no idea how to find it.

CHAPTER 5

GARTH'S FACE HARDENED as he pulled his long, muscled legs under the wheel of the white Mercedes. Merrily was soft, svelte, and desirable in the front seat beside him, but she felt glittery and cheap after what happened. He cast her a cold side-glance, jaws clenched. Merrily recoiled painfully in response to his dark expression. Trembling, she stared down at her hands.

She wanted him to hold her, tell her that he was sorry he'd brought up Mark again. At the same time, she wanted him to feel what she was feeling at that moment. She'd tried every trick she knew to attract him. But Mark was always between them, a shadowy, unpenetrable wall. Still tense, she watched as he started the motor and roared out of the parking area in the direction of the Main bridge.

If only there'd been time for him to court her before the wedding. He hadn't wanted to waste time on a courtship though. Those days could be better spent as man and wife, he'd said. Maybe he intended

to court her during the Aspen honeymoon. But now
. . . His tanned forehead wrinkled. She wondered
what he was feeling.

He must have sensed then that Merrily was watching him. He stole a glance at her. He seemed to be
able to tell even when he didn't turn to her.

Garth reduced his speed in order to cross the river
bridge that led to their home. With a squeak of
brakes, the car slowed, then eased onto the bridge
. . . thumping loudly as one by one the tires hit the
speed traps.

How she'd dreamed of him holding her during
those years that separated them. More than once in
her marriage to Mark she dreamed that Garth drove
to Houston and simply carried her away with him.

But he could never do that. His moral code kept
him away. He told her that when they began writing
after Mark died. Yet even when he put an ocean between them, he was never out of her thoughts.

Mark's death at last gave him the chance to find
her again. But he'd been too eager. He should have
given her more time.

Slowly, he loosened his hold on the wheel, but it
changed nothing. His emotions still appeared to be
tied in knots. If only Merrily could untangle them.

He always said that he never wanted anything
cheap with Merrily. She was his ideal, his Rachel.
Yet he cheapened them by acting as he had all evening. She wanted, no, needed, to forgive him, but
couldn't.

He seemed to be trying to calm himself. Merrily
shot him a curious glance. Did he want to kiss and
make up?

For an instant he averted his eyes from the road
and glanced at her, caught and held the moist brilliance of her blue gaze. Briefly she opened her
mouth, she wanted to tell him how she felt but

couldn't. She turned away and looked down the winding road ahead. They were growing further and further apart.

Merrily choked back a silent plea for help. She was losing Garth, and there was nothing she could do about it. She'd seen that haunted look before. She longed to reach out to him, hold him as she held Todd and Suzan when they were hurt.

No! That wasn't the way she wanted to hold him. It wasn't the way she wanted to be held either. She wanted . . . Oh, what was the use?

Her nerves were shattered. She had to do something, make up a shopping list. *Anything* to forget her problems if only temporarily.

Garth wheeled the curving road, but his thoughts still centered on Merrily. She'd calmed down slightly, as he had, since their verbal battle ended. Or was she merely pretending?

"Women!" Rick Webber had said that morning at the base.

Garth smiled briefly to himself, remembering the look on the young man's face. He'd been honored, as Rick's superior officer, that the kid had shared his marital problems with him. In a moment of weakness Garth even promised to help him get back with his wife, then wished he hadn't. How was he supposed to help Rick? He couldn't solve his own marital problems.

The shocker came, however, when Rick informed him that his young wife was none other than Helga Gerber, the German girl who was at that moment caring for little Suzan and Todd. Had Helga been married when he took her to the movies with Tom and Inga that time or the time he took her to the picnic? She was just a kid. He thought of her in just that way, simply killing time until he could marry Merrily.

77

Rick and Helga had married secretly, he'd learned from Rick. She retained her maiden name. Now Rick wanted to declare their marriage and take her back to the states with him. Yet Helga refused. Garth wondered why.

He slowed and turned, inching the car into their dark garage, then glanced over at Merrily with a guarded expression.

Inside, her heart thumped wildly, but Merrily was determined not to show it. Placidly, she followed Garth inside. When they stepped into the entry, Garth closed the door and locked it. Merrily crossed to the stairs.

She was part way up the stairs, trembling and misty eyed, when Garth caught up with her and touched her hand. She turned. The look in his eyes mesmerized her senses. She couldn't look away. In that moment, she forgot all the bitter things she'd been thinking. Her eyes reflected back the tenderness she felt for him. His face was wrapped in a shroud of what she perceived as frustration and deep pain. If only she could be sure that those were the emotions she saw there and not total disinterest as she so feared. Was there a trace of loneliness in his dark eyes, too? She'd been lonely after Mark died. Only Garth's letters from Germany were able to wrench her back to life again.

All at once she wanted to see him smile, to wipe away all the hurt and loneliness she saw etched in his face, but she wasn't sure she could manage it. She forced the corners of her mouth upward. A smile burst forth then, from deep inside her, showering him with warmth.

He watched her a moment through suspicious eyes. Then her smile broke down his defenses.

Slowly a hint of a grin took form, turning up his lips a trifle, bringing new lights to his handsome face. Still smiling, he offered her his arms. She hesitated, then fell into the circle of his arms.

"I'm sorry, honey," he said almost humbly against her ear. "I didn't mean to hurt you."

Enchanted, she wanted to believe him. Still, a part of her resisted. Why did she find herself half scorning the thing she desired most?

He removed the combs, allowing her long, dark brown hair to cascade down her back below her tiny waist. Tenderly, he kissed a spot below her right ear. Her sharp intake of breath appeared to drive Garth wild. He pulled her even closer. His breathing deepened. His mouth traveled slowly toward hers. She felt once more all the wondrous sensations she'd learned to expect. His lips captured hers. She responded eagerly, surprising even herself. At last, he released her. Arm in arm, they climbed to the top of the stairs.

"Will you take the baby sitter home now?" she asked softly.

"Merrily!" A glimmer of devilment glowed in the dark depths of his eyes. "You wound me deeply." He held his hand to his heart in a playful gesture. "Here I was playing Romeo to your Juliet, and all you can think of is trying to get me to take the baby sitter home."

The feigned innocence she saw lurking in his eyes melted away the rest of her bitterness. It was replaced by a tickling desire to laugh out loud.

"Garth!" A soft giggle assaulted the silence as she pushed him toward the door to the children's room. "Get out of here and take the sitter home!"

In fun he allowed her to push him dangerously close to the doorway, but no farther. Though she continued to shove with both hands, he wouldn't budge. He stood, one arm propped against the wall, and smiled at her with an amused expression that

Merrily found adorable.

"Think you can make me, huh?"

She pushed again. "I can try."

"How?"

"Oh, look!" she exclaimed, pointing toward the window at the end of the hall.

With a look of astonishment, he relaxed his muscles just long enough for Merrily to get in a good shove. In an instant he was staggering in the darkened hall just outside the door. "That's how, Cap'un," she said in her best Scarlet O'Hara voice. "But if you want to hear the details, you'll just have to take the sitter home first." She lowered her lashes in a teasingly inviting gesture. "And I can assure you, Cap'un, I'll make it worth your while."

"Always happy to please, ma'am," he said with a Rhett Butler wink. Still grinning, he gave her a bow. "Especially for a lady and one as pretty as you."

"And don't forget, Cap'un, you'll need to pay."

"Pay?" He shot her an amused smile complete with the allusive dimples. "Pay who?"

"The sitter, of course!"

"Oh yes," he went on playfully. "The sitter. The little German girl."

"The teenage bombshell. Tom's girl's little sister in case you've forgotten. And her name's Inga, I mean . . . Helga."

His smile broadened as if he was greatly amused. "You mean *that* baby sitter. Well now, in that case, I guess I'll be off." He ambled to the door, opened it, then looked back over his shoulder with a glint in his eyes. "Are you sure you can trust me alone in the car with a teenage bombshell?"

"About as far as I can throw you!" she said as she slipped into their bedroom and shut the door.

She heard him laugh, then knock on the door to the children's room. Helga opened the door, whispered something, and stepped out into the hall. After a moment Merrily heard the clop clop of wedge heeled shoes as Helga preceded Garth down the stairs.

They were in the car and Garth had just brought the motor to life when Merrily remembered that Garth had gotten a phone call just before he arrived home from the base that evening. A PFC Rick Webber if she recalled correctly. She usually remembered to tell him of all personal calls. How had she forgotten this time?

Soon Garth would return after taking Helga home. He would be charming, funny, romantic, exactly as he'd been just before he left. Smiling, she moved across the room toward the antique armoire, removing her blue dress as she went. She tossed it on a chair.

A diaphanous white gown came to mind. Opening both carved doors at once, her hands searched among the line of clothes for its delicate softness. Garth liked her in white, she reminded herself with a satisfied smile, and dreamily she removed her night gown from the plastic hanger.

Garth shifted uncomfortably behind the wheel of his sports car, afraid even to glance over at Helga for fear of encouraging the girl again. If he didn't know better, he would swear that she was actually coming on to him. Flattering as the prospect might be, he had no intentions of starting anything with Inga's little sister . . . and Rick Webber's wife, he remembered suddenly. Oh, boy! Now he'd done it. He'd promised Rick that he would talk to Helga, help him get back together with her. How was he going to accomplish that small feat? He needed to lay the groundwork first, let Helga know that he had no intentions of . . . who did he think he was anyway? Don Juan? He probably only imagined that she had a "thing" for him. He chided himself, *how con-ceited can a guy get? She was merely being polite to her employer. That's all.*

She'd been chattering, trying to involve him in conversation, since they left the house, and all he could remember about it was that she spoke English much better than her sister did. Helga hardly had a German accent at all.

His thoughts were squelched when Helga leaned toward his side of the front seat, drowning him in the pungent aroma of her strong perfume. Softly, she said, "I saw that picture of Mr. Knight tonight for the first time. He was a handsome man, wasn't he?"

Garth froze. "What picture?"

"The one in the children's room." She paused, as if trying to analyze his shocked expression, and moistened her lips with deliberate slowness. "I was surprised to see that you would allow it. Not every man would let his stepchildren put up a shrine to their dead father. But it's obvious that you're a notch above the average man in many ways, I think."

Garth gripped the wheel. Every nerve he had coiled. "What do you mean, *shrine?*" he demanded in a loud voice.

"Well, I didn't know what else to call it." Her voice trembled a little. "Actually, it's more of a tribute table, I suppose, the kind you might find in a library or a public building. I saw one like it once."

Scowling there in a darkened car, he tried not to raise his voice again, let Helga know of the anger her words conjured. "Would you mind explaining what you mean, Helga?" When she didn't answer, he went on. "Describe this so-called shrine for me, will you?"

"Well, as I said, it's not really a shrine. It's just a small table with Mr. Knight's picture on it, some old letters, and a photo album. That's all."

Garth tensed. A harsh expletive rippled through his brain, but he didn't say anything. *That's it,* he thought. What more proof did he need? Now he knew exactly where he stood with Merrily.

There was no so-called shrine with *his* picture on it anywhere in the house. He'd never even seen the picture he sent Merrily when she was in Houston. No doubt she'd hidden it away somewhere or tossed it out with the garbage.

His mind was a maze of conflicting thoughts and emotions.

"Captain Butler," Helga said, drifting into his thoughts once more as if she was speaking from far off. He was aware that she'd been talking, but he had no idea what she said nor did he particularly care. "Captain Butler! Please say yes, because if you don't, I don't know what I'll do."

"Oh sure, Helga," he said automatically, reaching into his pocket and handing her the usual fee for baby sitting without really looking at her. "Whatever you want."

They'd reached her house, he noticed, and she was preparing to get out of the car. Glancing back, she said, "Until tomorrow then."

Startled, Garth snapped to alertness. "What about tomorrow?"

"You promised to meet me at The Löwin at five o'clock so we could discuss my problem with Rick." Her pouty tone infuriated him. She sounded more like a scorned lover than a baby sitter. "Surely you haven't forgotten already." She blinked like a little girl about to cry, waiting for his answer. "Say you'll be there."

Nervously Garth gunned the motor, still refusing to meet her eyes. "Yes, I'll be there, Helga. I said I would, and I will. You can count on it."

Garth never went back on his word even when it was to his advantage to do so. That was part of his charm: loyal, true, trustworthy, helpful. He'd made a magnificent boy scout as a kid growing up on a ranch in North Dakota. But was he making it as a husband?

The vision of Mark's picture haunted him. It was almost more than he could bear. Merrily must have known of the so-called shrine to Mark Knight's memory. The children wouldn't have come up with something like that on their own. She probably put them up to it. He pictured her dusting it, looking at it, kissing . . . He had to stop battling the ghost of Mark Knight. There was nothing unhealthy about Todd and Suzan wanting a picture or pictures of their late father in their room. So why did the thought hurt so much?

Helga Gerber Webber smiled with satisfaction, then pushed back a tuft of golden hair. She was standing in the doorway of her apartment complex watching Garth's white Mercedes roar on down the street in the direction of the Main bridge, but her mind was busily planning her next move. So, she'd been right in predicting Captain Butler's reaction to her announcement about Mr. Knight's photograph. The smile widened.

Even girls much less perceptive than Helga would have noticed how upset he was on hearing the news. Perhaps he was thinking that Mrs. Butler put the pictures there for reasons that had nothing at all to do with her children.

Arms crossed over firm young breasts and leaning against the door frame, Helga glanced up thoughtfully at a sky of blackest velvet dotted with a thousand stars. If the pictures suddenly disappeared, then what? Wouldn't the ravishing Mrs. Butler think that her husband destroyed them? Helga laughed smugly to herself. Who else but Captain Butler would have a motive for doing such a thing? A giggle escaped again. Who indeed?

Still smiling, Helga closed the door and locked it, then climbed the stairs to her parents' second floor apartment. Yes. She would go to the United States as the wife of an American soldier. But perhaps instead of going as the wife of a PFC, she would go as the wife of an army captain.

Garth turned the corner automatically, his thoughts still centered on the picture of Mark Knight that was at that moment scorching what seemed to him to be unmendable holes in his shaky marriage. How could he ever have thought that Merrily was his Rachel? The lover of his dreams. The realization was shattering.

Rachel. That was what his Uncle Ted called Garth's *real* mother, Cary Rachel Thomas Butler. Though, of course, Garth had never known Cary, he'd always felt he did through the glowing accounts of her he heard from his uncle, Major Ted Thomas of the United States Army.

Cary had been a deeply spiritual, Christian woman, according to his uncle. Uncle Ted had, whenever possible, coached Garth through the years in the things he felt Cary would have wanted her son to know about the Lord of Abraham, Isaac, and Jacob. But the major had not visited the ranch as much as Garth would have liked. His stepmother, Monique, never made Ted feel welcome.

"Your mama was a beautiful, saintly woman, Garth, like Rachel in the Bible," Ted always said. "And when you marry, I pray that you'll find your Rachel, too, like your papa did. That kind of love will last a lifetime. But only if God joins you together. He's the link that keeps the chain from breaking."

Merrily drifted downstairs and into the darkened entry hall with a heavy heart. The feeling of joy she'd felt when Garth left to take Helga home quickly faded on further reflections. Unconsciously she rolled back the top of the stained, oak desk and began straightening Garth's papers with shaky fingers. Their marriage wasn't working out, as she'd always dreamed that it would. Making up hadn't changed that. The revelation suffocated her. Garth was right, she thought. They needed to go off for a holiday alone together. Still she knew that was impossible with two small children to care for at home. How did other second marriages survive the challenge?

Suddenly she remembered the sign she'd seen in front of the little church in Houston the morning after their wedding. *A family that prays together, stays together.*

It sounded too simple, like something Shelly would say. Shelly had certainly been badgering her lately to, as Shelly put it, find the Lord. Well, she had found Him, years ago. Merrily went to Sunday school and church as a child; she felt that it was important that her children do the same. What more could anyone ask?

"Are you a believer in Jesus Christ?" Shelly had asked.

"Well, sure, Shell. Who isn't?" She recalled feeling a little defensive at that point. Did Shelly Trenton think she had a patent on faith or something? "I'm a believer just like it says in John 3:16." Shelly probably didn't know Merrily knew that verse, and she felt a little smug saying it. "I went to Sunday school and was even a member of the junior choir. How about that?"

86

"I'm sure you did, just like I'm sure that you believe your doctor when he tells you you've got the flu and that you need to go to bed, take medicine, and drink plenty of liquids. But do you believe the Lord enough to do what *He* says to do in the Bible? That's what a believer is, you know, someone who believes God, not man. The Lord told us all, in the Bible, exactly how to live our lives to the fullest. But most of us ignore what God says and do our own thing."

"Does that include you, Shelly?" Merrily said sarcastically. "Or are you already perfect?"

"Absolutely not. If it wasn't for grace, I'd be headed for a nose dive. But I'm headed for heaven, Merrily, because I accepted God's free offer of salvation through grace and faith in Jesus Christ. And you can, too, if you give your heart to Jesus and allow the Holy Spirit to guide your life."

"There you go with another of your famous catch phrases, Shell. *Give your heart to Jesus,*" Merrily mocked. "Can't we ever talk about anything besides what a rotten person I am?"

"You're not rotten. You just don't know who your Lord is yet. I used to be the same way. I followed manmade philosophies while calling myself a Christian. I thought I was great because I dropped the kids off at church on Sunday. But now I know that a true believer seeks God for answers . . . not Sigmund Freud, a horoscope, or something like that."

"And I don't seek God. Right?" Merrily snapped.

"Only you can answer that question, Merrily, I can't do it for you."

Obviously, Shelly thought that Merrily wasn't a believer or she wouldn't have brought up the subject in the first place. Merrily liked Shelly. She was a good friend. But when Shelly got on that religious soap box of hers, Merrily wanted to strangle her. As if a few prayers would heal her ailing marriage. Merrily knew well enough what *would* help her marriage survive. Being truly alone with Garth. Her problem was doing it.

She'd almost completed her rearranging job when she heard the hum of Garth's Mercedes as it rounded the curve and eased down their street. Quickly, she completed her task and rolled down the desk top. She would bring up the idea of them taking a holiday without the children as soon as Garth arrived. Finally setting a date was sure to sweeten things between them even if they couldn't actually get away for a long time.

CHAPTER 6

GARTH HAD INTENDED TO IGNORE Merrily that night, after what he'd just heard. But she was waiting downstairs in her white, satin robe when he got home.

She dazzled him with her dark, ethereal beauty. But he tried to pretend otherwise. The playful mood he'd been in when he left to take Helga home had vanished. By the look on her face, Merrily's playfulness had disappeared, too, and he wondered why.

"What's wrong, Garth?" She appraised him a moment before turning back toward the stairwell.

A muscle tightened in Garth's jaw, there at the bottom of the stairs. He could see her clearly with moonlight streaming in from the French doors. Rejecting her was agony. Why did she affect him this way? Why did he always end up wanting to make her smile?

"What's bothering you?" she asked again with a sob in her voice. "Is it me?"

"You?" His emotions responded instantly to the

hurt he saw in her lovely face, but his mind refused to acknowledge it. He was remembering Mark's picture and how desolate the thought of it made him feel. "You're the marriage expert, Honey. You tell me."

A soft cry rose from her throat and seemed to hover above them. He felt like a rat, hurting her like this, but he couldn't forget what Helga said. He kept hearing it replayed inside his brain. To hold her now would be like begging for Mark Knight's leavings. He could never do that. He had a small measure of pride even if he hadn't shown it lately.

At last Merrily spoke, dissolving the curtain of silence. "If you'd just tell me what's wrong, Garth, I'm sure we could work it out."

Garth laughed mockingly. "Wrong? What could possibly be wrong?" His deep, cutting voice held a coldness that even managed to slash away a part of his own emotions, not to mention Merrily's. "But I would be interested to know why you put up a shrine to my predecessor."

"Put up a shrine!" she exclaimed loudly. "What in the world are you talking about?"

"The little table set up in the children's room, Merrily, the one dedicated to the memory of Todd and Suzan's late father. What else?"

"But I can expl . . . " Merrily's voice cracked with emotion. "Explain about that."

"Don't bother! It's perfectly all right with me. I couldn't care less."

"But I care!" she shot back angrily. "And it isn't what you think, Garth. I had nothing to do with it!"

"That's a little hard to believe since Todd and Suzan are barely out of the crib," he said coldly. "Are you trying to suggest that they set up the whole display without your help or knowledge?"

"Certainly not!"

"Well then," there was a tone of dismissal in his voice. "Need I say more?"

"Yes," she exploded. "I mean no! . . . Because I have a lot more to say, and I'm not about to shut up until you've heard me out. And don't think you can stop me with more of those slicing inflections that you so cleverly slip into your voice whenever the need arises, because that won't do you one bit of good. You're going to hear me out, once and for all, and that's final!" Her voice as well as her face had heightened, both in color and pitch. Blue eyes glistened in a wash of new tears. It pained him to witness it. Then, as if she could hold back no longer, the well broke, and Merrily crumbled into a fetal coil of uncontrolled weeping.

Garth had felt her trembling body as she brushed by him and sank down onto the brown tweed couch. He longed to take her in his arms and comfort her.

The heart wrenching cry of a wounded woman had never made sense to him. Nor did it now. Still, it touched him, and he wanted to console her as he longed to be consoled.

Monique, his stepmother, cried like that. Suddenly, he could almost see Monique's dark, scorching eyes.

Unpleasant memories choked him. He wanted to wipe away the memory of his stepmother from his brain forever, thought he had. So why was he recalling them now?

But Merrily wasn't Monique, he reminded himself. She was nothing like her.

His situation was exactly the same though. To Monique, Garth was second best. After all, Roger was her natural son. And with Merrily, he was also second best after . . .

Watching Merrily now, he could almost believe she cared. Automatically he reached for her, then stopped himself just in time. "Go on, Merrily," he said. "Let's hear the rest of it."

"No!" she shot back angrily and sprang to her feet. "I won't!" Suddenly her voice took on a polite coldness that was far more cutting than all her emotional outbursts. "I won't go on because you don't care, Garth. You never have! You've already judged me guilty of numerous unnamed crimes. So it doesn't really matter what I say." She paused, hands on her hips. "Does it?"

"Maybe not." He tried not to let Merrily know that her words had hit the target. And he began to understand a little of how she must be feeling. "Still," his voice softened slightly, "I'd be interested to hear what you have to . . ."

"No! Not on your life!" she interjected swiftly. "You'll get no more explanations from me!" Enraged, she turned haughtily and shot up the stairs.

"Okay, Merrily," he shouted after her. "Have it your own way."

Garth turned toward the living room with clenched jaw, hoping to drown himself in something light on German television. But concentration escaped him. The TV was a blur. He kept remembering Helga's words and wondering, unwillingly, what Merrily had intended to say.

When he finally went up to bed, he dreamed of his beautiful dark haired Rachel, Merrily. He smiled in his sleep as his dream progressed.

She moaned softly in her sleep, turned toward him. All hostile thoughts vanished. In her sleep she was Rachel. Moonlight encased her in shades of gold, highlighting the dark mass of long, shimmering hair that had suddenly captured a part of his pillow.

Careful not to wake her, he pulled her into the tender warmth of his arms. Holding her again, he slowly savored the sweet freshness of her. She was all he ever wanted.

If only she needed him as he needed her. Lightly, his mouth brushed her creamy forehead; then he buried his face in the gentle aroma of her long, near black mane and whispered love words that he'd never say when she was awake. He was holding her in just that way when sleep finally enveloped him.

When the alarm sounded the next morning, they were still entwined. Merrily had molded herself even closer to him as they slept, he noticed, and it pleased him enormously. Her long hair fell like a dark, raven cloud across his chest. It tickled a little he thought with a smile. Slowly, he breathed in the clean scent of her hair before carefully removing it in preparation for his daily journey to Group Headquarters.

He rose stiffly, stretched, and quickly dressed in the chilly darkness. The only light beamed from his small, pocket flashlight. Silently he left the room and crossed the hall. He'd already reached the top of the stairs when he remembered Mark's picture.

He wanted to see it, *had* to see it. The thought of Mark's picture enshrined in his home would eat at him constantly until he'd seen it for himself. He might as well see it now rather than allow it to spoil his day.

Guiltily, he slipped inside the children's door and shined his flashlight all around the silent room. Under the windows, he saw something, a small, wooden table centered by . . . He moved the light in closer. Yes, there it was, a black photo album and a photograph in an antique, gold frame.

Moving still closer to the table, he felt painfully threatened. The gray eyes of the man in the picture seemed to follow him, watch him. *A handsome face,* he noted with a cold tenseness that was suffocating.

Garth would remember every detail of that photograph, those haunted gray eyes for the rest of his life. He needed only to look at little Todd or Suzan should he forget.

He stared at the picture a moment longer, then turned toward the door and shined his light. He heard Suzan call out softly in her sleep as he left the room, and he turned back to comfort her. *The poor little kid was probably having a nightmare.*

"Go back to sleep now, little sweetheart. Uncle Garth's here," he whispered. Garth kissed Suzan's cheek lightly, then tiptoed out of the children's room and into the dark hall.

* * *

Someone was banging on the front door downstairs when Merrily finally opened her eyes much later that morning. She'd been dreaming of Garth and hated to wake up. Then bang! The awful racket floated up again from downstairs.

Merrily covered her ears against it. *There should be a law against early morning callers,* she thought, as she rolled out of bed, reached blindly for her white, silk robe and matching slippers on the chair beside the bed.

Sleepily, she peered around the room for the combs she'd worn to the reception. At least they would keep her hair out of her eyes until she managed to answer the door. Her blue gaze fell on Garth's pillow where their heads had rested. Merrily felt a gentle warmth. She'd awakened during the night, found herself in his arms, and snuggled closer to him. Too sleepy to remember their fight, she enjoyed it. A soft tingle lighted her on recalling the moment.

The banging started again, cutting into her sweet

reflections. Angrily, she snatched up the combs that had fallen beside the bed. She was still putting them in place as she raced across the room and down the stairs.

The children were already at the door when Merrily finally let Helga inside. *Helga,* she thought jarringly. She couldn't even remember asking Helga to come in that morning. Merrily was still too groggy to consider the matter further.

Helga's huge green eyes, that exactly matched the knit shirt and pants she was wearing, laughed back at Merrily from just inside the door. Still in her robe, Merrily felt a rush of self-consciousness. Helga probably thought she was a lazy slob.

"*Gutten Morgen,*" Merrily said, forcing herself to sound not only German but glad that Helga had arrived. Then she turned, closing and locking the door. "Nice to see you, Inga, I mean Helga. Please forgive me for calling you by the wrong name. I have a problem with names, especially before my morning coffee."

"Good morning," Helga shot back in flawless English. Merrily turned back around. "Isn't the day beautiful?" Helga paused and studied her as if she'd just noticed that Merrily was still in her robe and slippers. "Oh!" Helga slapped her own cheek lightly and glanced briefly at the ceiling in a gesture of pretended surprise. "I'm sorry. I don't suppose you've been out yet, have you?"

"Not yet I'm afraid," Merrily replied stiffly. Then, in nervous frustration, she tried to bolt the front door again, causing another moment of chagrined silence. "I usually try to dress before I go out."

"But of course." Helga peered at Merrily an instant longer, as if she were sizing her up for a future boxing match, then turned and smiled down at the children. "So what shall we do today?" she asked them with mock excitement. "Make cookies? Or . . ." She deepened her tone of voice playfully, "play castle in the dark and dangerous cellar?"

"Both!" the children said together, clapping their hands with enchantment.

She'd leaned down to their level, Merrily noticed, exactly as all the best books on child care say to do. Merrily was convinced that Helga would be a success at any task she attempted. Was there no limit to the girl's accomplishments? She was asking the children which game they wanted to play first when Merrily tuned-in to their conversation again.

"Let's play in the cellar first," Todd suggested.

"Yeah!" Suzan echoed, grabbing one of Helga's hands and pulling her forward while Todd took the other. "And let's start right now."

"Hold it!" Merrily clapped her hands loudly. "Nobody's playing anything until we've washed our faces and had breakfast." She directed the children toward the stairs, then turned back to Helga. "You can start in the bathroom, Helga, as soon as we've finished in there, then clean the bedrooms while we have breakfast. Later, I want you to help me unpack some things I bought for the kitchen."

"Very good, Mrs. Butler," the blonde girl said with a tinge of sarcasm. "But I have to leave early today because I have a five o'clock appointment in town. At The Löwin," she added with emphasis as if she wanted to make sure that Merrily heard the name correctly.

Merrily paused and frowned, digesting Helga's words, then followed the children up the stairs.

Right after lunch Garth called from the base to say that he wouldn't be home for dinner. He had an appointment, he said, in town. Funny, those were the exact words Helga used.

Helga left at a little before three in order to bathe and dress for her five o'clock appointment. *Appointment*. There was that word again. Could Helga and Garth be meeting at the . . . ? No, of course not. Helga was just a child. And there was certainly no cause to think such nonsense about Garth either, she reminded herself. She was being silly, allowing her imagination to run wild.

By 3:30 Merrily decided that she'd had enough of staying indoors. She and the children would dress, leave the house, hike across the Main bridge, and do a little sightseeing and shopping in town. Later they could have supper at . . . The Löwin. And why not at five o'clock? She wouldn't exactly be spying. Anyone had a right to be there.

Sundown came earlier in Volksheim than in some other cities in Germany. The town was surrounded by hills. It was often shadowy by five now that fall was near. Garth wouldn't like them being out after dark.

She paused, considering her options. They could take a taxi home. No problem. But was she really being honest with herself? Was her need to be out of the house the real reason she wanted to go out for dinner? She had to admit that it wasn't. She needed to prove to herself that Garth and Helga weren't together. Her friend Shelly hinted once that Inga wasn't her problem; it was Inga's little sister, and she couldn't go on wondering if maybe Shelly was right.

Gathering the children and herding them across the living room floor, Merrily's mind was everywhere but on the stairs just ahead. Suddenly she noticed that they'd been playing there again. There was a toy on almost every step.

"Okay troops!" she demanded, a hand on each

narrow hip. "Who left toys on the stairs?"

"He did!"

"She did!" the children said together, each pointing to the other.

"Well, it looks like we've got two guilty parties here. So I strongly suggest that you two get to work right now and put everything away. And I don't *ever* want to see toys on the stairs again. Okay?"

"Okay, Mommy," they said without expression.

"Good! Now I'm going on up to lay out your clothes." She started up the stairs. "And I want these stairs in tiptop shape. Otherwise," she paused for emphasis and peered down soberly at them from the top of the stairs, "no trip to the toy shop. Okay?"

"Yes, Mommy."

"Yes, Mommy," echoed Suzan.

Merrily entered the yellow and white bedroom for the first time that day with an amused smile. She'd actually managed to worry them a little. Were her children finally taking her scoldings seriously?

Suzan's handiwork, a funny, yellow, homemade clown hung on the wall beside Todd's drawing of a cowboy. Seeing them there, looking so sweetly childlike, almost made her exhausting day worth it. Crossing the wooden floor with a creak of old oak, her eyes swept the room carefully. She started to open the built-in clothes closet that Garth had especially built for the children, when she paused, suddenly puzzled. Thoughtfully, she glanced around the room again. Something was different. Something was out of place or missing.

The two, German-style single beds and Helga's cot were neatly made and dotted with yellow pillows. The toybox stood in the corner, opened, and with toys spilling out, as always. A low, white table and two matching chairs rested on the yellow rag rug.

The antique rocker that the landlady left in the house when they moved in was intact. The table under the double windows was . . . Mark's picture. Her heart pounded. Where was it? The children would be crushed. Where could it possibly . . . ? Garth!

Instantly she remembered his harsh, thrashing words of the night before. A burning rage ignited in the center of her being. He'd talked about the "shrine" she was supposed to have erected. The nerve of the man.

Her whole body tensed on remembering. Garth must have destroyed Mark's picture. It seemed incredible. Yet it had to be him. Nobody else had a reason to do it. But why? Was it wrong for Mark's children to have a picture of their late father in their room?

Feeling faint, Merrily sank down onto the old, wooden rocker and held her head with both hands as if to block out her thoughts. The whole scene devastated her. There had to be another explanation. But she wasn't at all sure one existed.

CHAPTER 7

AT A LITTLE BEFORE FIVE Merrily ushered her children into The Löwin and followed the little man in short, gray, leather pants to a small table away from the band and near the kitchen. She sank down into a small, carved, oak chair with a fatigued sigh and stacked her purse and packages on the floor by her side. The children scuffled gaily across from her on a wooden bench. A cold stare from her side of the table was required to hush them. Purposely she'd taken the chair facing the door in order to watch for Helga. Or Garth, she thought coldly. Her whole body strained against the on-slaught of stinging thoughts: his possible rendezvous with Helga, the missing picture. It was all too much to digest at once.

Blinking her eyes in the hope of exorcising the jumble of riddled thoughts that kept hammering inside her brain, Merrily reached for the large, white menu the waiter handed her with a mechanical smile. "Thank you," she said, sounding pleasantly detached and without looking up. "But we'll only be ordering drinks for the time being."

"But of course."

The waiter was watching her closely. She sensed it. His choppy, German accent held a note of concern that caused her to glance up finally in spite of her "downed" emotions.

"Excuse me, please," he went on. "But vot is da matter? Your eyes. Day say dat you are most sad. Is dare anything I can do?"

Merrily started to pretend that he'd only imagined that something was troubling her. But his pale, blue eyes were filled with such sympathy and a catching warmth that she felt a sudden need for candor.

Still forcing a smile that obviously hadn't reached her eyes, Merrily took a deep, regenerating breath. "You're very kind. And there *is* something. I'm not feeling my best this evening, and I might have to leave in a hurry." She glanced briefly toward the entry, then smiled back at the waiter again. "Is there another way out of here?"

"Yah!" He reflected doubtfully; then he nodded. A smile slowly lighted his broad, reddish face. "Through da kitchen." He pointed to the door around the corner from the wall display of steins. "If you must leave quickly, tell da cook dat Otto sent you. Yah? Her name is Crystal. She is my frau, you see, and she vill help you. I vill tell her of you and your *Kinder* here." He grinned down at Todd and Suzan. "She vill help."

Her blue eyes questioned him. "I could pay what I owe to your wife then?"

"*Nicht.*" His gray head shook. Briefly he narrowed his eyes. "It is not necessary dat you pay me today. I remember you from last night, and I can tell dat you are a good frau and a good mama. Pay vhen you are feeling better. Yah?"

"Thank you. And again, you are very kind."

"It is you dat is kind, smiling and saying such nice things to an old man." His laugh burst forth with such gusto and warmth that Merrily joined in in spite of everything.

She ordered Cokes for the children, nothing for herself. It would be best not to order dinner until she determined whether or not they were staying.

Smiling across the table at Todd and Suzan, Merrily casually glanced over their heads just as Helga strolled in. Looking young, breathless, and innocently seductive, Helga wore a skintight, yellow sweater that caught the gold of her hair and a tight brown tweed skirt. The matching tweed shawl tossed carelessly over one shoulder looked charming as well as designer perfect. She'd heard that Helga made her own clothes, but she hadn't expected them to be so smashing.

Pausing briefly under the huge, carved lion's head above the door frame, Merrily could see why Helga had chosen The Löwin. Every man in the room was watching her. Helga was truly a lioness at that moment, stalking her prey with pure animal magnetism. Merrily felt a pang of jealousy. Garth would think Helga was dazzling.

Hiding behind the menu that she held like a shield, she charted Helga's progress across the crowded room by the looks on the faces of the men. Merrily didn't know that she'd gotten even more appreciative male stares when she and the children stepped inside.

She felt shabby by comparison in a pair of old, faded blue jeans, a long-sleeved, blue plaid blouse, and an equally faded blue denim vest. She would have worn something else. The children insisted, however, that she dress exactly like them. It pleased her to allow them to have their way. She needed their approval, especially after the jolt she'd just gotten. She badly needed an ego builder.

Glancing quickly over at Helga's table, Merrily wondered who and where her escort was. *Garth,* she whispered mentally, praying it wasn't him. She glanced at her watch. It was past five, and Garth was rarely late. Her eyes gleamed with new hope. Maybe Helga's appointment was with someone else. Maybe her suspicions about Garth were unfounded.

With a smile, Merrily watched as Otto put two Cokes down on the table and winked at the children. Sighing softly, she thought over the situation as the children enjoyed their drinks.

She would have to tell Garth the news. Her nervous fingers drummed the hard, polished table. The children would notice that the picture was gone. When they did, he'd know. She hoped to introduce the subject mildly, not start a fight with her husband. She had no notion how to go about it, however. Almost any subject provoked a quarrel, it seemed. The missing picture was likely to ignite an explosion. She didn't plan to accuse him, just state the facts calmly and let things happen. Yet she was not certain she could stay with her plan if Garth were in one of his dark moods. A mental picture of his black eyes hurting behind a blinding fury flashed before her. He drew out the hidden poisons in her. She appeared to affect him in the same way. Would he believe the truth if he heard it? It hardly seemed likely if his recent history were an indication of his probable response.

Having Mark's picture on a table in the children's room was an idea created and perpetuated by Mark's mother soon after his death. Merrily saw nothing terribly wrong with it at the time; she allowed it in Houston without a word. It kept Mrs. Knight happy.

That in itself was worth the effort. Yet she'd never intended for the practice to continue once she married Garth. Mrs. Knight had been sly, however. Crafty. She'd convinced the children of the idea of having a table with Mark's picture on it in Germany behind Merrily's back, then told her of the plan in front of them at a weak moment for Merrily.

At the same time she'd been thinking about how she'd loved Garth while married to Mark. Her mother-in-law's words had cut deeply into the guilt in her heart as if in answer to her lusty memories.

"The children so want to keep on having their father's pictures in their room when they get to Germany, Merrily," Mrs. Knight had said smugly. "Surely you won't try to stop them; will you?"

"No. Of course not, Mother Knight," Merrily had replied rigidly. "I wouldn't dream of it."

Then Merrily listened in silence as Mrs. Knight explained to Todd and Suzan exactly how to set up the table in their new room in Germany. Actually, it reminded Merrily of a "how to" course in marriage wrecking. Mrs. Knight had not been pleased to learn of Merrily's plans to wed Garth Butler.

"I'm sure they know how to do it," Mrs. Knight had added. "But should they have a problem setting up the table and pictures, I'm sure you'll help them out; won't you, Merrily dear?"

She'd nodded in agreement like a wooden puppet. But she should have protested. She knew that now. At the least she could have warned Garth of what was to come. The truth was that she'd forgotten the incident completely in the excitement of the wedding, her new life. Maybe she was unconsciously hoping that Todd and Suzan would forget about it, too.

They'd suggested putting up the table in their room as soon as Helga arrived though, the night before. Merrily recalled that Helga eagerly set it up while Merrily bathed in readiness for the reception at the base.

Something made Merrily glance up from her reflections. Garth strode into the darkened restaurant looking handsomer than she'd seen him in days. Stung deeply, she noticed that he was holding his German pipe. He couldn't smoke it in front of Merrily. The smell made her sick. Would he smoke while dining with Helga? If he were meeting her, of course. Would Helga share a part of him that she never could?

Her blue gaze clouded, following Garth to Helga's table. She wanted to look away, but she couldn't. If he glanced her way, he would see her watching, know she'd followed them. She had to look away, get away. Yet her body was welded to the chair.

Then Helga called his name. "Here, Garth," she said from across the room.

Merrily's world suddenly shattered. Despondently, she wrenched her eyes from *their* table and regarded her children with pretended excitement. They'd finished their drinks, she noticed. There was no reason to remain at The Löwin any longer.

"I'm feeling *much* better now," she said, pretending an air of exuberance. "And wouldn't it be fun to eat dinner at the Wolksheimer?" She saw the disappointment gathering in their large gray eyes and decided to try a little harder. "We've seen all there is to see here. And I know Frau Languth will be thrilled to see you two again."

They sighed loudly and exchanged bored expressions.

"Maybe her grandchildren will be there this evening," Merrily added hopefully.

"Do you think they might be?" Suzan asked, wide-eyed with sudden interest.

"Maybe. Who knows? Would you like to find out?"

"Yes!" Todd jumped up and started for the door. "Let's go!"

"Hold it, Todd." Merrily whispered a little louder than she intended. "Come back here. We're not going out through *that* door. Remember? . . . Otto, our waiter, wants us to meet his wife. Out in the kitchen."

"Oh, yeah, I forgot," he said as Merrily rose resolutely from the table.

Garth felt someone watching him as soon as he sat down at Helga's table. But Helga kept him so occupied, pretending interest in her conversation that he didn't have time to look around. He finally noticed as Merrily and the children got up and headed for the kitchen. *They probably went to the rest rooms.* Their table backed the kitchen wall. *They'll be back shortly,* he thought with confidence, gazing down at the menu.

He planned to invite them to their table, then drive the family home and forget Helga and her problems with Rick.

Helga had to go. He couldn't allow her to continue in her position as their family baby sitter after the overtones she made last night in the car and now in The Löwin. If Helga really wanted his help in getting back with her husband, she had a strange way of showing it.

Turning back to Helga, he felt her leg brush his under the table in a way that could hardly be called accidental. A bolt of indignant rage exploded quickly, from deep inside him, reddening his neck and face. How could he ever have thought she was a child? With one lifted brow, he moved lithely to the empty bench on the other side of the table.

106

He'd only sat on the bench beside Helga because he wanted to make sure that their conversation remained confidential. Now, he didn't care who heard. He wanted nothing more to do with Helga or her marital problems. Rick would have to ask the chaplain or someone else for help.

Garth couldn't hide his irritation. If the chaplain couldn't help them, he would suggest they consider consulting "Dear Abby" or some other person of that stamp. He didn't really care what they did as long as he was no longer involved.

Oh, where was Merrily? he thought, glancing nervously toward the kitchen again. Had one of the children fallen in?

It was an effort, but Merrily and her children managed to get through dinner at the Volksheimer with Frau Languth . . . minus her grandchildren. Todd and Suzan had been terribly disappointed that Annetta and Khristoff were out of town for the day. And when the good Frau asked Merrily where Garth was, she almost choked on a fish bone. By the time the taxi pulled up to their door, Merrily had a headache that only a good cry could cure, a luxury she couldn't yield to in front of her children.

Seeing a light on in the attic apartment next door, Merrily had a strange urge to visit her new friend Polly Stardard. Polly would cheer her up.

Their blue Volkswagen was missing from the garage, Merrily noticed. That meant Bob had duty on the post and Polly was alone. It occurred to Merrily that Polly was probably almost as lonely as she was at that moment. Even Todd and Suzan couldn't ease it. So why did she think Polly could?

"Why don't we be neighborly?" Merrily suggested to her children. "Let's go visiting a while before we turn in." She'd already moved a few steps up the red, brick walk leading to the house next door.

"Come on! Don't be wet blankets."

"Visit the landlady? Yuck!" Todd exclaimed. "She's a witch."

"That's not nice, Todd. Besides, I'm not talking about her." Merrily took them playfully by the hand. "I want to visit Mrs. Stardard. The one you call 'the pretty lady.' "

"Oh, her," Suzan put in with a smile, "she's nice."

"She gave us cookies this morning."

"How nice. I hope you remembered to thank her." Merrily smiled down at her children and they smiled back. She led them up the walk then and up three flights of stairs to Polly's tiny, one-room apartment. Standing in front of the door, Merrily rapped softly. "Polly," she called. "It's us, Merrily Butler and company."

"Oh, hi," Polly called warmly from the other side of the door. "Just give me a minute to clear away some of this mess. Okay?"

Merrily smiled to herself, instantly knowing exactly what that mess was sure to be. Polly was an artist and constantly painting or sketching a scene of some kind or other no matter where she was, and she'd warned Merrily about what to expect. Merrily pictured the one-room apartment with canvases and paints scattered here and there, a clothesline filled with Polly's clothes and Bob's uniforms hanging from wall to wall. And she was not wrong in her assumptions.

The slant of the roof made the attic room unsuitable even for a pair of midgets. It was a disaster zone for two tall adults. Merrily ducked under the clothesline that hung directly in front of the door like a long, detour sign, and looked up into the amber eyes of her tall, slim, sandy-haired friend.

Todd grabbed hold of a long-sleeved, green army

shirt and began to dance around with it as though it was still pinned to the line. Suzan took hold of the shirt next to it.

"Cut it out, kids," Merrily said automatically, scolding her children with a squelching gaze. "And behave!"

"Oh. Leave them alone." Polly's usual vibrant and carefree voice did little to help Merrily control her children. But it brightened her own dampened spirits considerably. "They can't hurt anything."

Merrily forced herself not to nod at Polly in agreement. The room overflowed with boxes, finished and unfinished paintings, and unironed clothes piled on the small, single bed that Polly and Bob shared under the dormer window. Merrily couldn't imagine how two adults slept in such a small bed.

A small, white painted table, two straight backed chairs, and a two burner electric hot plate on a narrow, wooden cabinet made up the bulk of the furnishings. An old-fashioned, black, coal burning stove was used for heating. The refrigerator was a small, cardboard box set outside on the window ledge in winter. According to Polly, they used the landlady's ice box downstairs in summer. It was all exactly as Polly had colorfully described it.

Yet in spite of the clutter, Merrily loved being there. A certain optimism and warmth reached out to everyone who entered. Merrily thought that the sparkle was mainly Polly herself. If anybody could bring Merrily out of the dark mood the last few hours brought on, Polly could.

"So what have you been up to, Polly?" Merrily asked. "Besides painting, naturally."

"Interviewing for a job," Polly shot back with a glimmer of a smile and took the other chair. "Of course I'd hate to give up all of . . ." she swept the cluttered room with a teasing gesture, "this," she said as she feigned a hopeless sigh and shrugged humorously. "But you'll have to agree that we do need a larger place, and an extra job would make that possible."

Merrily laughed. "Absolutely. So tell me about this . . . job."

"Not until I've poured you a cup of coffee. Sorry I don't have anything for the kids."

Todd and Suzan were occupied on the floor with a big book of paintings by the old masters. Merrily sighed with relief as Polly poured her a cup of instant coffee. "Now, I've been both served and made comfortable," Merrily said. "There's no excuse now not to tell me."

"There isn't much to tell, really." Polly sat back down with her coffee. "Bob told me about a couple of openings for subs up at the high school on the post. I don't qualify for a job as a substitute teacher. No college degree. But I do qualify as a substitute teacher's aide. So I applied and interviewed. Haven't heard anything yet, of course, but I'm hoping." She lifted her cup to her lips and took a sip of coffee before going on. "As you probably know by now, jobs for the spouses of U.S. Army personnel stationed in Germany are almost nonexistent. I'll be lucky if I get this."

"Darn lucky."

Merrily had completely ignored her coffee since hearing Polly's news. Wheels turned so fast inside her head, that she hardly heard the rest of what Polly said.

Jobs, she thought, *and at the school.* She'd given up hope of using her hard earned teaching degree since she decided to marry Garth and move to Germany. But now.

A picture of Garth and Helga together at the small

table at The Löwin flashed before her eyes. Merrily tensed, blinking away the image. But the thought remained. She would need a job of some kind if her marriage . . . She had to stop thinking like that. Perhaps it was all a misunderstanding. She owed it to Garth to hear his side.

Merrily didn't realize that Polly had stopped talking or that she was staring into space until Polly called her name. "Merrily! Where were you?" The perk, vital quality usually found in Polly's voice was replaced with quiet concern. "What's wrong? All anybody has to do is look at you to know something's the matter."

Merrily shook her head. "Oh, it's nothing. Really."

"Trust me?"

Merrily glanced toward her children, then back to Polly with a request for understanding. "Not now."

"Later then?"

"Maybe." Merrily forced herself to smile. "Now tell me about the other jobs at the school, the ones that require a college degree."

"Are you a teacher?" Polly asked.

"In a matter of speaking. When Mark, my first husband, died, I took part of the insurance money and finished my education at the University of Houston. I figured I'd need some way to support my two children, and I wasn't really qualified for anything except babysitting. My schooling was in elementary education. But soon after I graduated, Garth asked me to marry him, and here I am."

"And now you want a teaching job. But none are available at the moment, I'm afraid. I understand that they do need qualified substitute teachers. And, of course, women teachers are always having babies; so there's always the possibility that an opening might come up later."

"Fantastic! I think you've just given me the information and push I've been needing, Polly. I need an outlet, and I'll need something even more when school starts next month. Todd will be in kindergarten, and I understand that Suzan will qualify for their pre-kinder program. So as you can see, I'll have a lot of time on my hands in the near future."

"They're always needing Sunday school teachers at the base chapel, Merrily, if you're at all interested in that sort of thing."

"I'm really not, I'm afraid. Church and all that is great for kids but . . ."

"You're an adult. Right? Well, I know what you mean because I used to feel that way, too. I . . ."

Merrily hadn't realized, until that moment, that Polly was as religious as Shelly. But she'd had clues. Plenty of them. Suddenly, she wanted to bring up religious matters she'd never allowed anyone to discuss with her before. At the same time, she was afraid. Commitment to anything meant giving up something, and she wasn't prepared to give up anything at the moment.

With a sigh, she decided that the best course would be to change topics. "Shall we toast to kids then?" Merrily asked finally.

"Why not?"

Merrily smiled then in spite of her problems. She lifted her brown cup to Polly's with a click of plastic on plastic. "To teachers, children, and teaching jobs. May they never die out," she said, but her smile faded as her thoughts returned to Garth and Helga.

Garth had hoped to complete his business with Helga as swiftly and painlessly as possible, settle the matter once and for all, and forget it. But nothing was accomplished toward his goal of getting the young couple back together. In the process of trying,

Garth risked his own shaky marriage. He stiffened remembering. He waited in vain from his table at The Löwin for Merrily and the children to return.

At last, Garth decided to ask the waiter what happened to them. He was surprised to learn that they'd left through the back door. Had something gone wrong? More likely, Merrily was upset about Helga.

With a cold, "Goodbye," Garth hastily departed the table. The meal that he'd carefully ordered for the two of them hadn't even arrived. He paid for the dinners quickly and stepped out into the cool of early evening.

Shadows played on the reddish stone building that lined the street and on the cobblestones. Ignoring his car parked directly in front of The Löwin, he hurried down the street in the direction of the Main River at a brisk, heart-pumping pace. He had to get away before Helga had a chance to follow him. He needed to think before facing Merrily.

He was almost sprinting by the time he reached the river. Slowing to a respectable stride, he exhaled audibly as he skirted the rocky bank without really seeing it.

A long, flat tanker marked EXXON sliced the calm, icy waters. A chilling wave lapped across the top of his black, army boots. Kicking back at the wet sand reflectively, Garth stepped back from the river but only slightly. He could still feel the damp cool, hear the gentle lick of the waves splash to a foamy halt against the shore.

The tanker eased slowly on down the river, following the sun that was already hidden behind the hill that held the castle. However, Garth had no wish to chase after it. His thoughts remained in Volksheim, divided between a two-story house on the other side of the Main and an attractive, young, German woman who obviously wanted him.

Plainly, he had nothing to do with Helga's secret marriage to the young private under his command. Yet he did like Rick and had wanted to help him.

He never thought of his previous encounters with Helga as dates, the meetings that took place before his marriage. He'd never so much as kissed the girl. To him she was a child. But now. His brow wrinkled, recalling the unchildlike gazes she'd thrown him across the table earlier that evening.

Wishing to end a rather fiery relationship with her older sister, Garth introduced Inga to Tom Drake almost a year ago. Tom had indicated that he was interested, and Garth gladly obliged him. He'd even gone out with them as a threesome, at first, to break the ice.

To please Inga's younger sister, Garth finally invited Helga to go along, to make a fourth. Helga's friendship was pleasant enough. He wasn't interested in seriously courting anyone in Germany at the time. He was courting Merrily by mail.

He took Helga to a movie on the base and on a picnic, much as one might take a little sister out. He never dreamed that she'd taken it seriously.

Garth climbed up the slight embankment and sank down onto a park bench to watch as dusk claimed the river. Yet his thoughts still held him prisoner. Looking off toward the village, his gaze caught a church like the one he and Roger visited once with Uncle Ted. He loved his younger brother even after all the years of separation. But he didn't feel love for his stepmother. Maybe he never had.

Monique had been sweet to Garth at first, he recalled. She was probably trying to impress his father, but Garth thought his stepmother really cared. At three, he needed a mother's love, desperately. With childish eagerness, he gave her his heart.

Two years later, Roger was born. His birth signaled the end of any maternal relationship Garth might have had with his stepmother. Monique made it plain from the first that Garth was "out" and Roger was "in." But it was years before Garth completely stopped trying to recapture her love.

Through all his growing up years . . . knowing how Monique felt, Garth managed to keep close to Roger. Their closeness never changed in spite of Monique's indifference to Garth. Even now he missed Roger, Roger's young wife Pam, and Rogy, the nephew he'd never seen.

Unlike his brother, Garth loved cowboying and the ranch. He'd always been his father's choice to take over when Andrew retired. Roger was an artist. He had no wish to run the ranch. Still, Monique wanted the ranch for Roger, and she was willing to do anything to get what she wanted.

Seeing the problem, Garth's uncle, Ted Thomas, tried to help Garth by getting his nephew an appointment to West Point during his junior year in high school via a U.S. Senator friend. Garth was not opposed to soldiering. He had a lot of respect for his uncle who had made a career as an army major. But Garth's love was the ranch; it was all he ever wanted. Monique knew Garth planned to turn down the appointment. He tensed, glancing toward the river. *That was why she did what she did*. Garth remembered the lies his stepmother told his father about him. The years hadn't lessened the pain. Clenching his jaws with inner rage, Garth rose stiffly from the bench and ambled back down the street in the direction of his car, hands in his pocket. Monqiue's disapproving face haunted him. No matter how he tried, he could never completely erase it. His stepmother hadn't wanted him on the ranch and was willing to do anything to keep him from staying on as he'd wanted to do. Seeing the uselessness of trying any longer, he'd finally bent to the inevitable and accepted the West Point appointment.

Garth still didn't want to go home immediately. Unsure how to explain to Merrily about his dinner engagement with Helga, he wanted to put it off as long as possible. Telling her the truth appeared to be out of the question, for the present anyway. He couldn't break his word to Rick nor could he lie to his wife. Half truths never appealed to him. His keen sense of honor wouldn't allow it.

Slowly, he plodded back toward The Löwin. Helga probably left long ago. He'd been walking and thinking for over an hour.

Suddenly he was directly in front of the church he'd noticed earlier. He almost went inside. But in the end, he didn't. He didn't need that to solve his problems.

Merrily was asleep when he got home. Or, at least, she seemed to be.

CHAPTER 8

GARTH HURRIED DOWN THE STEPS in front of the snack bar the next afternoon and out onto the sidewalk. Helga attempted to corner him again and he was eager to get away. He wasn't in the mood for a rap session with Steve Allison either.

He saw Steve watching him as he tried to discourage Helga and knew that Steve was probably thinking the coast was clear for him to start something with Merrily.

Garth's jaw went rigid for a moment, remembering how he felt the night of the party at The Löwin when he saw Steve and Merrily dancing. Well he wouldn't allow it, not again. Maybe their marriage wasn't perfect. But it was a long way from dead. He increased his pace. But he wasn't fast enough. Suddenly Steve was racing beside him.

"Hey, Sir!" Steve began brightly, a smile slowly rising. "Where's the fire?"

Garth tensed. "I'm in a hurry to get back to my

office." He glanced coldly at Steve. "I've got a lot of things to do this morning."

"Unlike me, you mean," Steve finished and laughed nervously.

Garth gave the younger man a look that would have humbled a dinosaur. Yet Steve only smiled.

"I just ran down to the PX to see if the gift I ordered for my Mom's birthday came in. But it didn't," Steve volunteered. "I was about to leave when I saw you and . . . I saw you coming out the snack bar."

Garth's dark eyes challenged him to mention Helga.

"How's Merrily?" Steve tacked on.

"My wife's fine, thank you." Garth sounded curtly polite and wondered why he couldn't manage more control. The younger man was hardly a threat. Or was he?

"I'm glad Merrily's okay," Steve said. "I was a little worried. She seemed upset when you two left the party the other night."

Garth tried hard to control his growing anger. But he kept picturing Steve and Merrily dancing. He didn't know how much more of Steve's friendly patter he could take. "Do you always make such personal observations?" Garth asked.

"Only when it involves the people I care about."

Garth glared at Steve a moment, thunder gathering in his black eyes, but his voice still showed an unusual amount of control. "Meaning my wife, of course."

"Of course."

Furious at Steve's casual indifference to what he considered a major indiscretion, Garth stopped and spun around. A look of surprised shock radiated from Steve's eyes. But it did little to lessen Garth's volatile temper. He had a consuming desire to punch

Steve in the nose. His right fist balled in readiness, waiting tensely at his side. One more false move on Steve's part and his restraint would break down completely. Garth almost welcomed it.

"What was that again?" Garth growled finally.

"Sir?" Steve asked with a pleading gasp. "What was what again?"

"That line about your caring for my wife?" His fury intensified. "I want to hear more about that!"

People were watching; some were even hanging out of second-story windows in the brick building across the lawn. Garth could hardly attack an officer under his command right there in broad daylight. Still, the idea of doing it grew more and more attractive by the second. "I'm waiting, Allison!" Garth exclaimed. "Let's hear it!"

"Sir," Steve beseeched him weakly, "I really don't think this is the proper time or place to settle this."

"Then name the place and time, Allison!"

There was a brief, eruptive silence with both men glaring at each other. Then Garth slowly relaxed, and his hands dropped limply to his sides. With an audible sigh, Steve stepped back and away from Garth.

"You never did name the place or time, Allison," Garth said, almost calmly considering the battle that still raged inside him. "I think we should settle this right now; don't you?"

"How about over coffee at the club after work?"

"Fine!" Garth said dismissively. "But if you'll excuse me, I have to get back to the office." Turning, Garth straightened his already ramrod-straight back and shoulders and strode lithely back down the walk, leaving Steve far behind.

Garth took a cup and saucer from the serving ta-

119

ble, poured himself a cup of steaming coffee and ambled across the room. Self-consciously, he eased onto a heavy carved oak chair at a table for two in a quiet corner, feeling as if every eye were on him. The social room, as they called it, was small, smaller by far than the room used for large receptions and parties, but decorated in the same Old-World style. Garth would have felt quite comfortable there if what happened earlier hadn't occurred and if he were not waiting for Steve Allison.

He'd cooled down considerably since their hot confrontation on the sidewalk. He just wanted to get their talk over with so he could go home to Merrily. He hadn't wanted to tell her of the day's events over the phone, preferring to fill her in in person.

He was going to feel like a fool relating that he'd almost punched Steve Allison in the nose. She'd ask him why. And what could he say? That he got mad because Steve said that he cared about her. Even little Todd needed a better reason than that.

He lifted his cup thoughtfully. A little of the coffee sloshed over the rim and into the saucer before he put it to his lips. Why had he been so angry? And over nothing, really. He sipped the hot coffee slowly. Unconsciously savoring the smooth taste and smell, he pondered his next move. He'd been so furious. If he lived in another age, he would probably have challenged poor old Steve to a duel. At dawn, no doubt, and with Tom Drake as his second. He laughed inwardly at the thought. Now all he felt was overwhelming embarrassment.

Automatically, he raised his collar a little higher on his neck in an instinctive attempt to hide himself. However, there was a ring of truth in what he'd said and done, he rationalized. He didn't like Allison's attitude toward Merrily, and he planned to make that point perfectly clear from the start.

He'd just settled back in his chair after getting a second cup of coffee when Steve joined him with a cup of his own. They exchanged polite greetings. Again Garth had the feeling that every officer in the club was watching them. How did one go about apologizing for his asinine behavior and still make his point? Garth cleared his throat. That was as good an opening as any, he supposed with a shrug, and cleared his throat a second time.

"I owe you an apology, Allison." Eye to eye, Garth offered Steve his hand from across the table with an expression of polite formality. "And I hope you'll accept it. I made a complete fool of myself this morning in full view of half the seventh army, and I couldn't be more penitent."

Steve took Garth's hand, reluctantly at first, as if he were holding back with reserved fear. Garth pressed his hand firmly, then pulled back when he felt Steve's limp response.

Garth removed his hand, one brow lifted contemplatively. He studied Steve more carefully. He'd never trusted the possessor of a weak handshake. "I'll try never to let something like that happen again," Garth said with honest candor. "But I can't promise, you understand, until I know exactly what your intentions are with regard to my wife." Garth paused. "Would you mind telling me?"

Steve faltered, displaying a sort of half shrug. "I'm not sure I can, sir. I don't really know myself." He hesitated again. "Merrily and I go back a long way."

"So do we," Garth reminded him in a deep, sobering tone; his black eyes flashed briefly. "Quite a long way, in fact."

"I realize that, sir."

"And, of course, there's the fact that she's my wife."

121

"I know that, too, of course."

"But it has little to do with you and your feelings toward Merrily." Garth's dark eyes blazed, but his voice steadied and even deepened a little. "Is that it?"

"I'm concerned for her happiness, sir. She's a fine lady, and there's been talk around the base."

Garth's right brow arched sharply again. "And just exactly what is this talk that you refer to? Would you mind telling me?"

"Some are saying that you and Helga . . . That you and Helga Gerber are seeing each other."

"And if I assure you that is not true?"

"I would believe you, sir. Of course." He paused nervously. "Unless . . ."

Glaring at his opponent, Garth leaned forward in his chair so that part of his upper body invaded Steve's side of the small table. "Unless what, Allison?" Garth demanded.

Steve pulled back automatically, and glanced down at his untouched cup of coffee. "Unless Merrily told me something different," he mumbled under his breath.

"Are you in the habit of checking back with my wife for verification?"

Steve raised his head and returned Garth's gaze squarely. "No, sir."

"That, at least, is encouraging." Garth dropped his eyes and relaxed a little, reaching for his cup. "But you haven't answered my question concerning your intentions toward my wife by a long shot." Garth glanced up boldly again, clutching his cup. "And I want to hear your answer, Allison. Now!"

"I intend to remain a friend to her, sir."

"And just how friendly do you plan to get?"

Steve flushed briefly. "I'll honor her marriage—as long as there is one."

"But you'll be standing there in the wings ready if that should ever change."

"That's about it."

"Well, I admire your honesty."

"Thank you, sir." Steve paused nervously. "Is that all?"

"Yes." Garth exhaled loudly and took in a gulp of coffee. "I think that just about covers everything."

"Then I guess I'll be going."

Steve reached limply for Garth's huge hand. Garth took it doubtfully. Pressing it, he suddenly knew how the term "dead fish" originated.

* * *

September slipped in unobserved in the weeks that followed. Still Merrily never got around to mentioning the Bavarian vacation with Garth. The time was never right.

With Rick's blessing, Garth told Merrily why he'd been at The Löwin that evening with Helga. Merrily never mentioned the missing picture, however, nor did Garth tell Merrily of the memorable experiences he'd had while praying in the empty, German church. He'd gone there several times since that walk on the river's bank alone.

Merrily put the rest of her problems with Garth on a back burner, pretending that all was well. Of course, it wasn't. Her household was too involved with preparations for school to bother with anything other than clothes, supplies, and her new job as a substitute teacher.

One day the wooded glens that dotted the hillsides greened against the reddish stone and brick of the ancient buildings; the next they gloried in a symphony of fall colors. Yellow, red, gold, and burnt orange leaves whooshed on the backs of brisk, autumn breezes. Skirts billowed in response.

An aura of excitement surrounded the smiling,

pink-cheeked Volksheimers, inspiring Merrily as she went about her daily tasks. Temporarily, she forgot the emptiness she'd felt the night of Garth's meeting with Helga and allowed the harvest season to revitalize her outlook. She was still acutely aware that there was something missing in their marriage, however, and she still had no hint as to what it might be. With school starting and the hassle of new schedules and carpools, she scarcely had time to think of her own problems.

By October the children were well settled in their classes at the American school on the base, chatting incessantly about school doings and the October Fest. Sometimes Merrily merely lazed in her room, looking out occasionally at the panoramic spectacle of everchanging color from her upstairs window. Their house fronted the river, giving her an exceptional view. Often she hiked to the top of the hill, crowned by the castle, where she could see for miles around.

Coming from flat and muggy Houston, Merrily had needed time to become accustomed to the dry, cool air, the constant climbing. It seemed that every street in Volksheim was either going up or down. But she'd started to enjoy it.

The added exercise firmed her already slim body to a healthy glow. A sleekness of form increased her beauty and suppleness. An inner sparkle emerged that only added to her vibrant charm. Sometimes Polly escorted her on her daily jaunts. At other times she met Shelly at the base or in town for a shopping spree or lunch at the Volksheimer. Yet all these activities did little to quell the nagging worry that was never really out of her mind.

Once she almost agreed to go with Shelly and Mike to the church on the hill. But that was a cop-out. Only seeking the Lord when *she* needed Him was wrong in her mind. You either were a Christian or you weren't. If she ever committed herself to something as important as God, she'd do it with her whole heart like she did everything else. And she wasn't ready for that yet.

She still heard whispers about Garth's supposed encounters with Helga but tried not to believe them. Most of the stories came directly or indirectly from Dell, giving her a good reason to brush them from her mind. Still, whenever Garth called from the base to say he wouldn't be home for dinner, the old horror crept in again, and she suffered through another terrible evening until he came home.

She'd never brought up the missing picture since that night at The Löwin. She told the children that somehow their father's picture was misplaced. The silences and lack of openness within their marriage created enough of a void without turning the children against Garth.

They'd lost most of the humor and candidness that existed before they married, and she missed it. It was only on rare occasions that they briefly recaptured a part of it. Merrily missed, too, the closeness they had previously derived from those witty exchanges Garth was so famous for.

Garth also suffered from the new coldness. Though he'd finally explained, he knew that deep down she still believed the worst about that evening with Helga. It didn't help his case that he'd been thrown with the girl several times since then. On one occasion Rick asked Garth to meet with the two of them, but only Helga showed up. On two other occasions, Helga just materialized at Garth's table at the snack bar after work.

Once he was waiting for Merrily. Suddenly he was aware of someone, looked up, and there was Helga. She left only minutes before Merrily arrived.

He'd told both Helga and Rick more than once that he was not responsible for getting them back together nor was he available for counselling. Still, that didn't stop Helga.

Autumn leaves crunched under his heavy boots as Garth strode briskly down the red brick sidewalk that November morning toward the PX, savoring the cooling freshness and the scent of harvest in the air. Only a scattering of leaves still remained on the trees, all in variegated shades of brown or deep red. By Thanksgiving, the trees would be completely bare, skeletons of their former brilliance.

Garth hummed to himself as he hastened his pace purposefully, mounting the brick steps two at a time. It was Friday; he'd been paid, and he planned to order that cuckoo clock that Merrily wanted as a surprise, Christmas present. Along with the other gifts he hoped to obtain, she was sure to be pleased and that pleased him.

He didn't see the slender, fair-haired young woman on the walk who was speedily overtaking him or the dark haired beauty, farther behind, who had just rounded the corner of the commissary and started toward him. He was opening the heavy, oak door when he heard a familiar, female voice call his name, "Garth!"

He turned, expecting to see Merrily, then let the door slam shut. Pink cheeked and bubbling with life, Helga raced up the steps and joined him on the landing.

She wore a pale green jumpsuit designed to flatter. "Can you spare an old friend a cup of coffee?" she asked with a breathless air. "I've been wanting to talk to you."

"If you must."

He opened the door again, and Helga preceded

126

him inside. If he'd glanced back, he would have seen Merrily duck out of sight.

"Good morning, Mrs. Arkin," Garth said, tipping his hat to the attractive elderly woman.

The entryway was wide and crowded with soldiers. The door to the snack bar, across from the PX, was wide open. He could see Shelly alone at a booth near the door.

"Well, Shelly," Garth called, moving ahead of Helga again. "I just ran into Helga and now you. Mind if we join you?"

Shelly looked amused. "Not at all, if you promise to sign up for the church choir. Merrily tells me you have a nice singing voice. And I'm recruiting."

Garth smiled, then felt a wave of embarrassment when Helga sat down by him at the booth and across from Shelly. "You know Helga, don't you?"

Shelly smiled warmly. "Yes. How are you, Helga?"

"Fine, thank you."

"So what about the choir?" Shelly inquired. "Are you game?"

"Merrily and I don't attend the base church, Shelly."

"I've noticed. So I'll put both of you down for the choir." Her smile turned serious when she looked at Helga. "How about you, Helga? Wanta join?"

"Yes. Put me down. Please."

What a switch, Garth thought, *considering Helga's recent record*. But he didn't express his views. He knew he was in for a sermon from Shelly. The girl never missed a chance to "spread the good news." Yet even that was better than having Merrily find him and Helga alone at a booth together.

Her slender body rigid with inner wounds, Merrily stepped back around the corner of the building, out of view, and buried her face in her hands. The image of Garth, looking down at Helga, taunted her. She hadn't believed the stories she'd heard, hadn't wanted to until she saw them for herself that day in The Löwin. And now this. With a choked sob, the tears came. She couldn't seem to stop them. That morning she'd been ill again. The fourth morning in a row. Now the base doctor confirmed what she'd known for days.

Her breasts were increasing and at a faster rate than the other times. If Garth ever really looked at her, he would have noticed. Leaning against the cold, rough building, a heartwrenching cry escaped.

Her stomach gave a sickening lurch. The nausea. She'd been unable to stand at the meat counter and buy meat last time she shopped at the commissary. She'd not even planned to try it today. The look and smell of raw meat appalled her. Feeling faint, she'd had to leave the store with only half of her shopping done. Yet that was minor compared to the feeling she got on seeing Garth and Helga together. Her throat coiled inwardly. Her stomach churned, remembering.

She had to catch a taxi and go back to the house at once. The shopping at the PX and commissary could wait until another day. She needed to be alone, to decide what to do. Blindly, she half staggered down the sidewalk in the direction of the main gate. She hardly noticed when a car slowed, then stopped a few yards ahead of her.

"Merrily," Mrs. Arkin called in astonishment. "What's wrong, dear? You look like you've just seen a ghost."

Merrily stiffened her back in a useless attempt to pretend that nothing was wrong, but she failed completely in her effort to fool Mrs. Arkin. She hated having the commanding officer's wife see her looking so distraught. But there seemed no way to avoid it.

Merrily tucked in her stomach self-consciously. The blue sweater strained against her full, young breasts, making her tiny waist appear even smaller. She *felt* pregnant, and wondered if her condition were already obvious. She should never have chosen a sweater to wear with the heavy, blue wool skirt. She'd stick to blouses and boxy jackets from now on, remembering the stares she'd gotten on previous trips to the army post.

An expression of warm compassion mounted in the faded, gray eyes of the older woman as Merrily moved toward her small, blue, Fiat sedan. "Get in," Lilly Arkin said. Merrily obeyed instantly.

"You're in no condition to go home alone." Lilly eyed her with a sweeping gaze. She paused. "Are you pregnant?" she asked with a delightfully Southern accent.

Merrily nodded, wondering how she could possibly know.

"I thought so. I saw you leave the infirmary, and there's a certain glow."

Merrily and Lilly exchanged appraising looks for a moment longer.

"And I suppose you saw your husband talking to that little snip of a German girl?"

The gray eyes questioned her in such a gentle, motherly manner that Merrily had no wish to hold back anything. Nodding again, Merrily let her moist eyes stray to her hands folded tightly in her lap.

Lilly's gray eyes and gray, upswept hair blended fashionably with the soft, blue-gray knit sheath. She looked like an aging fashion model. Blue-gray eye shadow had been applied carefully. Gold bracelets and matching earrings blended perfectly and looked expensive.

"Does *he* know about the baby?" Lilly Arkin asked finally.

"Not yet."

"I thought not." Lilly grimaced and uttered a low "men are beasts" sigh. Starting the motor, Lilly pulled out onto the road again. Her eyes straight ahead, she continued talking. "Now, about what you thought you saw back there. I saw the whole thing and Garth is innocent to any major crime you might come up with. He didn't meet her at the PX. I don't think he wanted her there. And he ended up at a booth with Shelly . . . so nobody could get the wrong idea. I know because I watched and heard everything. But he might be guilty of a minor indiscretion."

Unhinged by her words, Merrily shot Lilly a questioning glance. "Minor, did you say?"

"Minor in that she was there, and he's an attractive man susceptible to flattery, if you catch my meaning." She glanced at Merrily briefly and turned toward the main gate, "Let's go for a ride down to the town and then to the country for a while. You need a change of scenery." In a blur Merrily nodded, then sat back and allowed splashes of fall to calm her. Thirty minutes later Lilly weaved up the hill and back through the main gate.

A quiet street lined with cold, white, well-tended apartment houses loomed ahead of her. A small playground separated each apartment. "Where did you'all spend your honeymoon?" Lilly asked in her gentle, southern drawl, breaking the long silence.

"Well," Merrily began haltingly. "You see we only had . . ."

"What you're trying to say is," Lilly interrupted, "that you didn't have a honeymoon at all. Did you?"

"Not in the usual sense." Merrily felt unusually

calm, considering the probing questions she was getting, and not at all embarrassed.

"Wouldn't it be more honest to say that you didn't have a honeymoon in *any* sense?"

"I guess so." Merrily paused thoughtfully. "But it wasn't Garth's fault," she added. "Not at all."

"I hardly thought it was. Men seldom try to avoid the honeymoon."

They'd stopped in front of the last apartment house on the block, but Lilly made no move to remove herself from the car. Twisting around in the seat in order to face Merrily, Lilly smiled with understanding. "You see Morgan and I had a similar problem when we first got married." Merrily felt her face show the shock of Lilly's words. "Like you," Lilly went on, "I'd been married before and was a widow and the mother of three small girls." Lilly paused and the smile broadened. "The girls and I unglued Morgan at first, I'm afraid. He'd never been around children, you see, and just being around me would have been bad enough after all those years of bachelorhood. But the four of us together were like a whole army conspiring against him. For a while I thought our marriage was doomed."

Merrily's eyes widened with unveiled surprise. "What did you do?"

"I found a friend who would take care of the girls, and then I took Morgan on a long, belated honeymoon."

"And did it work?"

Lilly smiled smugly and cast a knowing wink. "Well. That was twenty-five years ago. Judge for yourself. But that was only part of the cure. The rest was commitment to the Lord, Jesus Christ."

Merrily smiled back with a puzzled stare, realizing that Lilly was one of those "religious types," too.

Lilly chuckled under her breath. "Surprised?" she

131

asked, but didn't wait for a reply. Clutching the handle on the door, Lilly hesitated and turned back to Merrily. "Why don't I drop you off at Shelly's. I know what good friends you two are, and she should be home by now. I'm sure you have a million things to discuss and plan. But if you don't let me keep those children of yours at least part of the time while you and Garth go on leave, I'll never forgive you. My grandchildren are sprinkled all over the United States, and I miss them terribly."

Doubt tinged Merrily's lovely face as she pondered Lilly's words.

"Now don't try to back out of this." There was a command in Lilly's soft voice. "You owe it to your children to keep the family together as much as you owe it to yourself and your husband and your Lord. And the children will get along fine with me. In fact, I'll keep them the whole time if you will let me."

"But what about the colonel?"

"Morgan? . . . He loves children. We have four boys of our own, you know."

CHAPTER 9

MERRILY HAD HARDLY STEPPED inside her bedroom door when the phone rang. It was Shelly wondering if she'd gotten home all right. The thought of Garth and Helga at the PX was still hard to swallow in spite of Lilly's encouraging words and Shelly's assurances.

"I'm fine, Shelly. Really. And have a happy Thanksgiving.

"You, too."

Drained as well as tired, Merrily placed the receiver back in its black cradle and fell across the smooth, cool silkiness of their king-size bed. How would Garth take her news about the baby? She felt like crying. She wasn't going to though, merely because she now had an excuse with all those extra hormones flowing through her system. Would Garth be glad or angry?

A swift pang of self-pity mixed with homesickness engulfed her, remembering other Thanksgivings, her mother's cornbread dressing and pumpkin pie. She cried easily now, and the problems with Garth didn't help. Her mother and father never had problems when she was growing up. Theirs was the perfect marriage . . . or so it seemed at the time.

She tried to picture her parents kissing at the front door of their home like they always did when her father came in from the base. The thought of them kissing always comforted her as a child. She closed her eyes and tried harder to see them. Instead she got a flash of Garth and Helga, together in front of the PX.

Sitting up in bed, legs crossed Indian style, Merrily forced herself to look on the bright side. Lilly and Shelly thought she had a better than fighting chance to bring back their marriage. Both agreed, too, that she needed to get Garth off by himself for at least a week, and both were willing to keep the children. All she had to do was convince Garth of the idea. She'd decided to ignore their well-placed spiritual suggestions, however, in favor of the togetherness approach.

She remembered how disappointed he'd been about the cancellation of the Aspen honeymoon. But how did he feel about going somewhere with her now?

Her thoughts were cut off when a car pulled up outside. Rising from the bed, she shifted her blue gaze to the clock on her dressing table. Three-thirty. That would be the carpool. Was it already that late? She'd spent practically the entire day at Shelly's. The house was a wreck since she'd let Helga go. Pulling the waist band of her sweater back down where it belonged, she ran a comb through her long, dark hair, raced downstairs, and opened the door, forcing herself to smile and pretend that nothing was bothering her.

Todd and Suzan were wild with school news.

134

Smiling down at them, Merrily led them lovingly into the kitchen and poured orange juice into two, small glasses while they elaborated.

"Wendy Jackson has the chicken pox, too!" Todd began.

"Too?" Merrily cocked her head to one side as a warning light buzzed inside her head and handed the children their juice. "You mean there are more?"

"Well, Albert Mendez had it first and then there was Billy Summers . . . or was it Candy Myers? I forget which one, but anyway Wendy's home sick now and Victor Carson is still out."

"Nancy and Paul have it in our room," Suzan put in excitedly. "My teacher, Miss Brandon, says it's almost an epodermic."

"That's *epidemic*," Todd corrected condecendingly. "I know because my teacher said so."

"When did all this happen?" Merrily asked. "I substituted a little over a week ago and nobody was sick then."

Todd gulped down the rest of his orange juice and lifted his glass for more. "I guess it was right after that then." His gray eyes traveled to the cookie jar as Merrily poured more juice into his small glass. "Can we have a cookie?"

"*A* cookie, meaning one for the two of you?"

"No," Todd explained. "*Some* cookies, as in three each."

"How about one, as in one each?

His face fell. "Come on, Mom. At least give us two apiece."

Merrily smiled and took down the cookie jar from the shelf next to the stove. Her children were growing up, especially Todd. He was calling her Mom now. His conversations and interests had taken a giant leap since school started. Todd and Suzan hardly sounded like her babies anymore, she

135

thought, handing them their quota of two cookies each.

They looked so bright and healthy sitting there at the white kitchen table. A ray of sunlight slanted in through the open window, spotlighting a pair of blonde heads, matching red plaid shirts, Todd's blue jeans, and Suzan's blue denim skirt. She'd have to stop dressing them like that, now that they were growing up. Todd had already informed her that they weren't twins and that he hated dressing like a girl. Garth had taken his side.

How would they feel about her plan to go away with Garth to the German Alps for two weeks? She'd never been away from them for any length of time.

"How would you two like to visit with Aunt Shelley, Uncle Mike Trenton and their children for a while? I was thinking that since you were getting so grown up around here, you might like a vacation away from Uncle Garth and me?"

The children exchanged excited glances, then gave a rollicking "Yes," with one voice.

Merrily smiled. "Mrs. Arkin has asked that you visit her, too. I think she wants to take you to Frankfurt for a few days and spoil the daylights out of you."

"Can we go by train again?" Todd asked in animated tones. "Like we did when we came here!"

"I think that's exactly what she plans to do."

"Great! When can we go?"

Merrily laughed. "Soon. Very soon."

"Oh, Mommy," Suzan said suddenly, changing the subject. "I forgot to tell you. Peggy Potter has the chicken pox, too."

"I'm sorry to hear that," Merrily replied, wondering who Peggy Potter was. Did every child at the base have chicken pox now? Certainly her two had never had it.

That night Merrily brought up the subject of a possible vacation alone in the Bavarian Alps. Garth applauded it. For the next three days Garth and Merrily finalized the details. Lilly Arkin and Shelly Trenton were in charge of keeping Todd and Suzan. Polly volunteered to watch the house and keep Todd's newly acquired, pet frog, appropriately named Prince Disgusting. They were scheduled to leave right after the Thanksgiving holidays.

The night before they'd planned to leave, Garth and Merrily went out to The Löwin for supper and quiet conversation. A planner, Merrily had packed their bags and made all other arrangements days in advance. There were no pressing matters to take care of; they could go out without feeling guilty. Frau Languth would stay with the children until they returned from The Löwin. Early the next morning they would load the car, drop the children off at Lilly's and head south.

The tension between them had lessened since the arrangements for their belated honeymoon began. Garth wasn't late for dinner because of unexplained appointments, and things were better at least on the surface. Merrily attended a Sunday morning church service with Shelly, but she didn't feel a part of it. That was Shelly's thing, not hers.

After supper Garth led Merrily out of the crowded Löwin and down the same route he took the evening he almost dined with Helga. The nights were colder now. Each wore a heavy coat and black, furlined snow boots in readiness for the first snow yet to come.

Puffs of whitish steam burst forth with every breath they took, then merged into one, big cloud that hovered above them, as they whispered and laughed, heads together, in the chilly hush of night-

137

fall. The brush of cobblestones against crepe soled boots blended with the occasional crunch of a dead leaf or the snap of a twig. Lighted Christmas trees blinked in many of the windows along the way, proclaiming the coming of the yuletide season, and the smell of pine cones missiled waves of sweet memories through their brains of another Christmas seven years before.

Merrily's red wool coat and matching mittens pressed warmly against her tender skin. Briefly, Garth lifted her fuzzy, red ear muffs to whisper in her ear, and a chill raced down her spine. Garth's overcoat was heather brown and cashmere soft. Merrily loved the feel of it on her cheek when she nuzzled the warmth of one broad shoulder.

Crossing over to the park that fronted the river, they sank down onto one of the empty benches, provided by the city fathers, and snuggled close. The moon welded silver ripples in the slow rise and fall of the river. Merrily couldn't resist picking up a stone, tossing it in, and listening for the belated plop as it hit the icy water.

The next two weeks promised to be heaven, precisely what their marriage needed. She hadn't told him about the baby yet. That topic could create new problems. She was not quite two months pregnant anyway and not really showing except in the increasing size of her breasts. She would tell him at the proper moment, perhaps while on some snowy hill during their honeymoon trip. Things would be exactly as they should be by then. She sighed. He would be ready to listen. He'd want to be a father.

"Penny for your thoughts," Garth whispered, lifting her ear muffs again and planting a quick kiss on each ear.

She shivered, in response to the sweet assault, then jerked her head slightly away from his. "Stop

138

it!" She rubbed her ears with mittened hands. "That tickles!"

"That was the general idea."

"Besides, it's cold. You let in cold air."

"Let me warm them again then." He removed his gloves, both her ear muffs, and covered her ears with big, warm hands. "Isn't that better, Ma'am?"

"Much. But I don't think Scarlet and Rhett had this problem. It never gets this cold or snows in Georgia . . . or so I always thought. I've never actually been there, you understand. But it certainly never snowed in Houston while I was there, or in San Antonio."

"That's a lot further south though." His voice deepened and took on an intimate, husky tone. "But even if it doesn't snow in Georgia, we can pretend it does for our own purposes."

Merrily laughed musically and glanced up at him with an embarrassed smile. "And just exactly what *purposes* do you have in mind, sir?" she said in a slow drawl. "My mama told me to watch out for rakes like you."

"And just exactly what did your mama say about rakes like me?"

"That you and all rakes in general were out to get only one thing."

"Aha! Now we're finally making headway. So, suppose you tell me what rakes like me are out to get." He tickled the back of her neck with now chilly fingers, and she leaned forward to avoid them. "And please be specific," he added, tickling again.

"Why Cap'un Butler." She settled back against his arm, looking up into his eyes. "You shock me to the roots of my southern modesty."

He chuckled, feigning villainy, and got to his feet, pulling Merrily with him. "I suggest that we continue this discussion in the privacy of my bedchamber across yonder river." He gestured toward the river, then turned back with a grin. "Come, wench!"

"Oh please, sir," she begged with mock terror, pulling away from his grasp. "Spare me!"

Suddenly three old man who'd been sitting in darkened silence on another bench got up in mass and started for Merrily as if they intended to come to her aid. Garth whispered in her ear again. "I think we better cut the theatrics, Honey, or I just might spend our two weeks' honeymoon in the poky."

She laughed at the thought of Garth in jail. "Why Wedwick, dear," she faked loudly and as if on cue. "I think you've got your lines for the play down perfectly. And may I say that you'll make an excellent villain? Perfect casting, I might add."

"You, Ma'am, make an exceptional minx."

"But you must admit that the role of the villain was made for your wide and varied talents." They were on the street again, and the three old men were still watching them from a position just inside the park. "And I can hardly wait until the first performance," she said loud enough for the men to hear. "Too bad it's not scheduled to begin sooner."

"That can probably be arranged." Garth, puffing out mouthfuls of smoke after their hasty retreat, pulled playfully at Merrily who lagged behind. "Come, Minx, fame and fortune await us."

Merrily was still laughing as he practically pushed her on down the dimly lit street in the direction of his car. "Oh, Captain, you say the most romantic things."

"And you, Ma'am, say entirely too much, especially considering that those three old men are *still* watching. Your protectors, no doubt."

Merrily glanced back to see that the old men had

moved to the center of the street and were facing them, three dark dots spotlighted by the yellow glow of a street lamp.

Her spontaneous laughter caused a similar response in Garth. "I see what you mean," she finally managed. "And my protectors are moving this way, I see."

"Then I suggest we make tracks, Ma'am, and fast."

They were still laughing when they got to the car.

A light snow blanketed the top of their heads as Garth whisked a still giggly Merrily up the walk toward their rented cottage. *An excellent ending to the first half of a perfect evening,* Merrily thought, noting the falling snow. *And the perfect beginning to what was to come.* She stopped before reaching the porch steps and gazed around. It felt good to laugh for a change. Removing one mitten, she held out her hand, caught a thin veil of glistening snow, and pressed it to her lips. "Oh, this tastes so good," she said almost to herself. "I'd forgotten how cold it was."

Garth stopped, too, and watched her with an amused smile.

She didn't want her evening with Garth to end. Why couldn't it go on like this forever? "Want some?" She pressed her cold, snowy hand to Garth's lips and laughed when he licked her fingers clean of the remaining snowflakes. "I feel high," she said, slipping on her missing mitten and emitting a bubbly laugh. "I'd think I was a little tipsy if I'd had so much as one drink tonight. I guess I'm high on laughter . . . like some silly schoolgirl, no doubt."

Garth had reached down and was scooping up a handful of snow. "The ability to play, like you do, is a sign of emotional maturity." He grinned. "Or re-

141

tardation." He was teasingly molding the mixture into a slushy snowball. "Hadn't you ever heard that?" he asked, glancing briefly in her direction.

"No." She eyed the snowball warily. "Then according to your prognosis, I guess we're mature. Right?" she asked with a whimsical laugh. "Almost to the point of senility."

"Or just plain crazy," he added, grinning widely and aiming his snowball at her with a playful expression. "Whichever one applies."

"If you're thinking of testing my maturity level by throwing that . . . weapon at me, you have another . . ."

She stopped in mid-sentence on noting the gleeful, almost devilish glint in his laughing, black eyes. "You wouldn't!" she exclaimed, shielding her face with her arms.

He let go of the snowball suddenly, and it hit her shoulder with a splatter of white on the red wool coat. "Yuck!" she shouted with pretended distaste. "I'll get you for this!" Reaching down with both fuzzy, mittened hands, she balled up a snowball of her own. Swiftly, she aimed for his head and detonated.

He dodged too late. The snowball exploded on impact in the curly darkness of his black hair, aging him instantly with a wet cap of melting whiteness. In retaliation, Garth scooped up a particularly sloppy handful and aimed it menacingly. "Ready to give up?" he asked playfully. "Or do you want more of the same?"

Instead of answering, she picked up a handful of her own and sent it sailing.

"I assume you want *more*!" he said, letting go of his snowball with a force that equalled hers. "And I always *aim* to please." Without giving her time to make a counterattack, he gathered up another batch

142

of the messy mixture and started toward her. "How about a nice slushy with a little mud and grass mixed in?"

He appeared to be about to plop the dripping mess in her face, and she turned her head to avoid it, laughing continuously. "Oh please, don't," she begged. "Not the slushy! Anything but the slushy." He'd grabbed both her hands with one of his and held them firmly behind her back. The dripping snowball hovered only inches from her face. "Can you be bribed?" she asked weakly.

He grinned villainously. "That depends. What are you offering? I can't be bribed cheaply, you know."

"Would a kiss be payment enough?"

"That would depend on the quality of the kiss." He let go of her hands and took her in his arms, dropping the snowball to the wet ground.

"Would you care for a sample?" she asked breathlessly.

"I insist on it."

Her lips and her heart were suddenly entrapped in the enveloping splendor of Garth's embrace. His mouth moved demandingly on hers to ever higher spirals of passion, erupting swiftly to a consuming blaze. Her senses reeled in response to the rapture he invoked in her, and she had no wish to be freed from it. His lips felt as icy as the night air when they first brushed hers. Now they were warm and as tender as the look that pulsated from his dark, possessing eyes.

They were still in the small courtyard that separated their house from the house of their landlady. With moonlight shimmering on the new fallen snow, they were the main attraction, live drama for anyone who happened to be watching. Yet Merrily never once thought of it until someone called down to them.

"Hey, you guys!"

It was Polly, yelling from her third-story window in the house next door. Merrily felt herself blush as she pulled away from Garth's unyielding kiss and glanced up in Polly's direction.

"Don't you two have a bedroom to go to or something?" Polly asked teasingly. "You've got the whole neighborhood panting."

"But it's snowing," Merrily said defensively, as if that explained everything. "You and Bob should come down here and sample a little of some of this. The more the merrier."

"What was that again?" Bob put in with a deep chuckle.

"Sample a little of . . ."

"You're talking about the snow, I gather," Garth whispered with an amused twinkle. "Or are you considering some sort of group sampling?"

"Does Bob think I meant that?"

Garth nodded.

A flood of embarrassment washed over her, on realizing what Bob must be thinking. "Maybe we should just go inside," she whispered back with an embarrassed laugh. "What do you think?"

"I think that's probably a good idea."

"We're going in now!" Merrily called up to Polly and Bob.

"It's about time," Polly called down to them.

With one smooth movement, Garth swooped Merrily up in his arms and carried her inside. "Garth," she said laughing. "What will the neighbors think?"

"That we're going inside." He grinned down at her. "I think that's indicated. Don't you?"

She nodded a breathless yes.

He set her on her feet again, and they were still laughing when Frau Languth shushed them worriedly at the top of the stairs.

Glancing up, Merrily's face sobered, stopping her progression on the stairs. "What's wrong?"

The older woman closed her eyes for a moment before answering. "It is Suzan. She is sick, very sick. Da fever is high."

CHAPTER 10

FEAR HUNG HEAVY for an endless moment, making it impossible for Merrily to move or think. Finally, she managed to break through it. With a muffled cry she bolted forward, attacking the remaining three steps with a vengeance, and raced inside the children's room.

Todd was resting peacefully in the single bed next to the windows. Suzan tossed and turned in the bed beside him, calling out in frenzied, unrelated monosyllables now and then in her delirium. Merrily dropped to her knees on the floor beside Suzan and softly stroked her feverish brow.

Slowly, she opened her eyes. "Mommy," the child cried weakly, "you're here."

"Yes, darling." Her voice choked with emotion. "Mommy's here."

"Mommy," Suzan spoke even more softly, "I don't feel so good. My supper came up and . . ."

"I know." Merrily patted her hand, then suddenly sensed Garth's quiet strength beside her. "And everything's going to be fine now."

"Mommy? Can I sleep with you in the big bed?"

Merrily glanced up at Garth, and felt a bewildered relief when he nodded with tender understanding. "Yes, honey," Merrily said, gazing down at Suzan and pushing back a stray curl that was wet with sweat. "You can sleep with Mommy tonight."

Merrily started to reach for her, but Garth already had Suzan in his arms, holding her close.

"Are you going to sleep with us, too?" Suzan mumbled half in her sleep.

"No, sweetheart," Garth said in a deep, gentle voice. "I'm going to sleep in your bed."

Still peering up at him Suzan patted his shoulder, her gray eyes half closed, and rewarded him with a vacant, fevered smile. "That's nice."

"I'll get you some clean sheets," Merrily put in, having a sudden urge to be useful. She jerked open the bottom drawer of Suzan's dresser, her voice shaking, and fumbled for the sheets. "I know they're in here somewhere."

Frau Languth stopped her, held Merrily's trembling hands firmly but gently, and smiled with wordless empathy. "I vill do da sheets, Frau Butler," she pledged at last. "You go now and be vith your *Kinder* and da sweet papa." She questioned warmly, "Yah?"

"Yah," Merrily agreed with an answering smile.

"Dat is good."

She followed Garth into their bedroom. She'd calmed a little by the time they got Suzan into bed and the child was sound asleep. But almost immediately Suzan started scratching her sores. There appeared to be an itchy spot on her head and another on her right thigh. All at once the words *chicken pox* ripped through Merrily's brain. Pulling back the covers, her gaze fell on a cluster of small, white blisters.

147

"Chicken pox!" Merrily exclaimed. "She's got it! There's no doubt. The whole school's infested with it." She glanced up at Garth. "You've had it, haven't you?"

He shrugged hopelessly and shook his dark head.

Merrily stared at him as if she hoped that she'd misunderstood. Chicken pox was a childhood ailment. Everybody got it in grade school. Didn't they? "You mean you haven't ever had it?"

"I'm afraid not."

She pressed her head with the palm of one hand, as if she half expected to drive away the thought, and a loud sigh cut through the hush of the silent room. The rest of the night was, for Merrily, a sleepless nightmare.

By the next morning both children were dotted with pink Caladryl lotion over small, itchy, white blisters. For the next two weeks, they both shared the king-size bed with Merrily. Garth "bached" in the children's room. The Bavarian vacation was scraped on the same heap with the Aspen honeymoon, then rescheduled for the week after Christmas.

A week before Christmas the children finally felt well enough to go back to school, but by then, school was out for the holidays. Shelly came to the rescue, however, and offered to keep them for the day. Merrily needed to catch up on her Christmas baking and a million other chores. She'd just put up the tree and had a pecan pie in the oven when Garth came home early from the base looking something like a warmed-over piece of white fish.

Excitedly, Merrily asked, "What are you doing home at this time of day? You look terrible."

"I'm not feeling well," he said, begging for sympathy with a typically male, helpless stare. "I have a fever and a bad headache." He paused and tried to smile. "Will you stay with me in the big bed?"

"Do you itch?"

He nodded weakly and scratched a spot on his middle, through the green army shirt. "But you didn't answer my question."

Merrily smiled in response to his vulnerable expression, ignoring his question. "Did you put anything on your spots?" He was a little boy and hurting, and it was her job to make it all better. "Well, did you?"

"You slept with Todd and Suzan when they were sick," he reminded her, feigning a little boy's voice.

"Have you taken anything?" she asked, choking back a smile at his one-track mind. "Anything at all?"

"No."

"Not even aspirin?"

He shook his head palely. "I keep telling you, all I need is to have you hold me for a while." He was trying to be funny, even with a fever. "Would you care to see my spots?" he asked, grinning.

"Go on upstairs, Captain, and take off your clothes. I'll be along with the aspirin and the Caladryl lotion in a few minutes. I'll take a look at your spots then." She paused, watching his apparent lack of comprehension. "Okay?"

"Okay." He turned, as if slightly disoriented, toward the stairs. "If you promise to doctor each and every spot with loving care." Then he glanced back at Merrily, inquiringly. "You'll be right up then?"

"You got it."

"I'm thirsty."

She pointed toward the top of the stairs and smiled encouragingly, but he continued to stare at her as if he were unable to move. "It's that away," she reminded him cheerfully. "Up." She gestured with her thumb. "Forward. March."

"Oh, yeah." He turned and attempted to stumble up the stairs.

Taking pity on his helpless, fevered state, she draped one of his huge arms across her shoulders and assisted him in mounting the remaining steps. "Come on. Let's get you to bed, and I'll bring you something to drink."

"How about freshly squeezed orange juice?"

"Forget it, soldier! You'll take the frozen kind or none at all. I've got work to do, and you've got a fever."

Her eyes shifted to a toy truck on the step just above them, a toy left by either Todd or Suzan. Merrily noticed it just in time to keep Garth from stepping on it. She stiffened; it could have caused an accident. Guiding his body around it, she gave herself a mental note to scold the children as soon as they got home.

Leading him toward the big bed, she felt his firm muscled body against hers. His fever was higher than she'd first thought. Why hadn't he stopped off at the infirmary before driving home? She wasn't a doctor or a miracle worker for heaven sakes. Didn't he know that?

"How do you feel?" she asked, easing him onto the bed. "Better?"

"No. Terrible! I need to hold you." He reached for her. "Come here, wench."

"Will you cut that out? You're supposed to be sick. Remember?"

She paused and grinned. "And you'll feel better soon. I promise." She removed his boots and unbuttoned his shirt. "Now. Isn't that better?"

"Not really. I still feel awful."

"Okay, baby," she said without a trace of sarcasm. "Now, just relax while I go down and get your juice. Okay?"

"Okay," he moaned. "But hurry. Will you? I think I'm dying, and I need mouth to mouth . . ."

"Don't you *ever* give up?"

Merrily tried not to laugh when she left the room. She did feel sorry for him. Certainly. But he was taking on worse than Todd and Suzan put together, and that I-need-to-hold-you-routine wasn't helping. She laughed to herself. This would prove to be a rather unique Christmas, to say the least, with Santa Claus laid up and freckled all over with pink lotion.

She gave him some aspirin and applied pink lotion to each and every blister. While he slept, she finished her baking and wrapped a few gifts. She was tying the last bow when the phone rang.

"Hello."

"Hello, Gorgeous. This is Tom Drake. How's Spot?"

"Who?"

"The chicken pox boy. We all figured that's probably what he had since both your kids had it."

"Oh." Her voice lost most of its vitality like it always did when Tom was around. "Garth's fine, I guess. And you're right. It's chicken pox. He's sleeping now though, and his fever is down a little."

"Can I do anything to help?"

His kind words struck a surprised but pleasant chord in Merrily. For the first time since she'd met him, Tom Drake sounded almost human.

"I can't do much," he went on, "but I can always run and fetch."

Merrily laughed at his countryish phrasing. "Running and fetching would help a lot, Tom. Could you manage to pick up Todd and Suzan for me at Shelly's?"

"Sure. When?"

"Right away if possible. I'll call Shelly and tell her you're coming."

"Anything else?"

"Well, if you could stop by and pick up some more Caladryl lotion at the PX, that would be a big help."

"So Spot is pink now."

"All over."

Tom laughed. "That figures. Now, how about you, Merrily? You must be half dead with the plague hovering over your home these last few weeks. What would you say if I got a couple of orders of fried chicken from the snack bar for you and the kids for supper?"

"I'd say thanks, and I accept."

"Great. Then I'll see you in a little while."

"Thanks, Tom. You're a pal."

"Am I really?" He laughed. "Well, it's about time!"

Hanging up after her strangely comforting conversation with Tom, her thoughts shifted instantly to his girlfriend, Inga, and Inga's little sister. She'd managed to keep Helga out of her thoughts since the children got sick. Yet all it took was one phone call from Tom to bring it all back again. *But Tom's acting like a real dear*, she thought as she dialed Shelly's phone number. Was he acting or was this the real Tom Drake? She didn't have long to wonder. He arrived thirty minutes later.

But Tom was not alone. Steve was with him. And Merrily had the strangest feeling that he'd come more to see her than to check on the health of his superior officer. When Tom left, Steve stayed on a while longer, insisting that a brisk walk back up the hill in the snow was exactly what he needed.

Garth opened his eyes, blinked, and slowly closed

152

them again. He didn't know how long he'd been sleeping. Hours maybe. The feverish, inner heat he'd experienced when he first went to bed had dimmed a little and the headache was gone. Still, he had an uncontrollable desire to claw every patch of skin on his dampened body. It would feel so good to scratch himself into utter oblivion.

His thoughts were interrupted when he heard a booming male laugh floating up from downstairs. His black eyes snapped open. He forced his fevered senses to sober alertness. Rigid, he strained to hear what was being said, and who was doing the saying.

"The children have been gone a long time," he heard Merrily say. "I think I better run next door, to Polly's, and check on them. She's probably going bananas by now."

"Don't," he heard the man say in an intimate voice. Garth's jaws tightened instantly. "Not yet," the man downstairs said. "Let them play a while longer. I need to talk to you."

"Now, Steve. Don't get crazy."

Stricken with a lash of instant fury, Garth shot out of bed, but a wave of nausea sent him right back in again. He tensed, fighting back both the sickening feeling in his stomach and the blinding rage he felt on hearing Steve Allison's voice. Steve was alone with Merrily now, and there wasn't anything he could do about it.

"There's nothing we need to say to each other that the children can't hear," Merrily said lightly to Steve after a long silence. "And I don't like the look in your eyes. So cool it, Steve. Will you?"

"Not until I've said what I came to say."

Garth tried again to get out of bed. But it was useless. Just forcing himself to listen to their conversation was difficult enough.

"I love you, Merrily. I always have," Steve said.

"And I'll be waiting . . . if you and Garth should . . ."

"Don't!" Merrily exclaimed. "Don't even think it."

"But I *do* think it, all the time."

"Stop it, Steve! I won't have it! I'm married to Garth, and don't you forget it!" She paused. "I think you better go now."

"But I haven't finished doing what I came here to do."

"I won't listen to another word!" She paused again. "Get away from me, Steve! We're not a couple of teenagers playing post office. I'm . . ."

Garth's stomach tightened, lurched tellingly. He wasn't sure he could even make it to the bathroom much less downstairs to rescue his wife. With a low moan, he jumped from the bed and staggered across the floor, his muscled body bent at the waist and tied in draining knots. His mind was downstairs. But his body heaved wrenchingly over the toilet bowl.

At last the first wave was over. He felt weak but better on returning to bed.

"I'm going now, Merrily," he heard Steve say, and an audible sigh of relief escaped him. Garth felt even better when he heard the front door slam shut. He glanced at the clock and smiled.

Slowly, he reached for the phone by his bed with pale, sweaty fingers and dialed his office. Rick would still be there if he called right now. The phone rang once. Twice.

"Captain Butler's office."

"Webber. This is Captain Butler."

"Oh. Hello, sir. How are you feeling?"

"Better, thank you. But there's something I want you to do for me, if you will."

"Of course, sir."

"I'm going to be laid up here at home for at least

two or three weeks. But I want you to reschedule my leave for as soon after that as you possibly can." He paused as the churning started again. "Have you got that?"

"Yes, sir."

"Good. And report back to me here at home as soon as you have a date."

"Yes, sir. I'll get on it right away."

Rick Webber waited until he heard a disconnecting click and dialed again. Helga didn't know about Garth's illness, and he'd promised to ask Captain Butler to talk with them again. He couldn't begin to understand why Helga insisted on a go between, and why only Captain Butler would do. He was too in love with his beautiful wife to care.

"Hello," Helga said with mild interest.

"Honey, this is Rick."

"Oh." She sounded slightly agitated. "What is it?"

"It's about the captain."

"Oh." Her voice brightened. "Will he talk to us then?"

"I am afraid not. He has the chicken pox, just like his little kids did. Oh, and by the way, Shelly Trenton wants you to go to church with her up on the post Sunday. She asked me to ask you, special."

"Then he won't be going on leave right after Christmas after all. Will he?"

"Who won't be going on leave?"

"Captain Butler, of course."

"Oh, *him,* well maybe. He wants me to reschedule though. About three weeks from now."

"Have you any idea where they plan to go?" she asked.

"No. I wouldn't know that sort of thing."

"Would Tom Drake know?"

"Probably. They're best friends. Why?"

"I just wondered," Helga said sweetly. "Are you coming for supper tonight?"

"You know I am."

"Good. We can talk more about it then."

"Talk more about what then?"

"Going on leave somewhere together."

"Do you mean it, Helga? Will you go on leave with me as my . . . wife?"

"Maybe not that. I mean I'll be your wife in every way, of course, but we won't tell it then. It will be a sort of testing, to see whether we fit, whether I should go back to the states with you or not."

"Oh, honey, you're really considering going then, aren't you?"

"I certainly am. I've been considering going to the states for a long time now." She paused. "And I have no intentions of changing my plans."

Merrily almost ran up the stairs after Steve left. She didn't notice that she still carried the baby pillow Steve had given her for the new baby. The colonel must have told Steve through Lilly about her pregnancy.

She had to be with Garth at that moment even if he was still asleep. After Steve's kiss, she'd felt dirty. She hadn't wanted it in the first place, tried to avoid kissing him, then felt guilty. Nothing more.

Garth lay on the bed, awake and looking extremely pale.

"Are you all right?" she asked, flooding him with compassion.

"I'm okay, I guess. How about you?" His gaze jolted her with a flash of hurt behind the black, piercing eyes. "I heard voices downstairs," he said.

Did he know about Steve's kiss? she wondered.

"Anybody I know?" Garth asked.

"Tom and Steve were both here."

"But not together," he finished for her. "Isn't that right?"

He knows, she thought, wondering what to say next.

"What did Steve have to say?" he asked, looking at her strangely.

"Garth, I don't know how to tell you this but Tom, I mean Steve . . ."

"Steve tried to make love to you with me up here, sick in bed."

"How did you know?"

"My hearing's excellent, and this house, these plastered walls, are like a mini sound system. Hadn't you noticed?"

She fell into his arms and buried her head against his. "I'm so sorry. It wasn't my fault, but I'm still sorry. It should never have happened."

"It wouldn't have if I had more control over my digestive system," Garth interjected. "I would have stormed down those stairs and really let him have it. In fact, I might let him have it yet, once I'm out of this blasted bed."

She pulled back a little in order to look at him squarely. His face was flushed and hot. "Promise you won't make another scene," she said. "All he did was kiss me. Once. Only once."

"But it was a long *once*, wasn't it?"

She felt chagrined. "Sort of."

"I thought so." The yellow, baby pillow dropped on the bed beside him during their embrace. Then Garth was holding it, looking questioningly at Merrily. "Are you trying to tell me something?" he asked.

She smiled through her moist, blue gaze and nodded excitedly. "Yes."

Their eyes fastened with shared elation. "You mean it?"

"Yes, yes, yes," she said.

He took her tenderly in his arms again and kissed her. The yellow pillow rolled off the bed, hit the dresser, and ended up somewhere under the king-size bed. Neither of them noticed.

Helga left the church service she'd just attended with Shelly Trenton that Sunday night with mixed emotions. She'd already scheduled a trip with Rick to Berchtesgaden at the same time the Butlers would be there. To back out now would sound odd to Rick. He'd gone to so much trouble to arrange things exactly as she asked him to. But her original plan to wreck the Butler's marriage held no interest for her any more. She was too eager to restore her own marriage.

She clutched the Bible Shelly had given her close to her breast as she climbed the stairs to her parents' apartment. Another Helga had climbed those same stairs only a short time before . . . determined to destroy others. How different she felt inside now, how peaceful. She didn't quite know what was happening to her, but she liked the feeling whatever it was.

She'd agreed to go to church with Shelly and Mike again on Wednesday night, then backed out when she heard that Merrily might attend. She didn't want to see Merrily at church. She felt too guilty about what she tried to do. Next time she attended church she'd make sure that Mrs. Butler wasn't going. Perhaps she'd know more then. Maybe she'd even go to the front of the church and give her heart to the Lord.

Three weeks and four days later Merrily and Garth were in a quaint hotel in Berchtesgaden, West Germany. It had been snowing constantly since they arrived the day before, and there were no signs that the storm was lessening.

The heavy, gold, floor-to-ceiling drapes were open. From the bed they could see through the glass doors leading out onto their private terrace.

Majestic mountains beamed whiteness all around them. Merrily thrilled to the panoramic view. Glistening with snow, the hills seemed to scrape the sky with icy slopes and smooth, snowy valleys, filling the air outside with cooling freshness and the scent of sleeping pines.

Inside, the room was sweet smelling, cozy, and warm. A roaring fire licked at cedar logs behind a shiny brass grate. The double bed was massive and high off the oak floor, shrouded in brown and cinnamon colored feather blankets. The couple relaxing on top of the blankets were oblivious, however, to the aroma of burning cedar or the cooking smells that drifted up invitingly from the kitchen downstairs. They were together but separate, each reading. Garth wondered why their glorious vacation alone hadn't yet drawn them closer, as he was so sure it would.

Garth only pretended to read his magazine. His mind was unable to comprehend anything but his dazzling wife beside him in a white wool sweater and matching ski pants. She appeared enthralled in her reading. Yet he wanted to talk. This was his long awaited chance to court her, and he wanted to make the best of it. Why wasn't it working?

"I never got a chance to ask you how you liked the church service you attended with Shelly and Polly just before we left. How was it?"

"Fine." She continued reading.

"Just . . . *fine*? I thought you would have more to say than that. You've gone with them several times lately, I noticed."

She glanced over the top of her paperback book

curiously, as if she wondered why he brought up the subject. "I felt out of place. That's all."

"Out of place?"

"They're both into religion, and I'm an outsider. I probably won't go again."

"Why don't you become an insider?"

"I wouldn't know how."

"According to my Uncle Ted, my real mother was an . . . insider."

Merrily smiled. "You never mentioned *her* before. Tell me about her?" She put down her book.

"There's not much to tell. She died when I was born. But my uncle said that she was very close to God."

"I wish I were," Merrily said candidly.

"I wish I were, too," he agreed.

The crack of a log in the grate startled her momentarily; she went rigid for an instant as sparks exploded against the screen. Patches of light filtered through the gold colored lampshade, highlighting the silky darkness of Merrily's hair with red and scanning the fine bones of her face.

With a deep sigh, she turned back to Garth. "What were you saying about your mother?"

"I finished talking about her. How about a discussion of another mother—you."

"Are you really glad about the baby?"

"You know I am." He smiled. "What would you like to do now? We could go for a walk downstairs or stand around and watch the snow fall. Which is it?"

"Read."

"Read?"

"I'd like to finish this book Shelly gave me."

Garth shrugged and picked up his newspaper. "I never thought I'd be jealous of a book. A paperback at that. What are you reading?"

"*The Rapture* by Hal Lindsey."

"Find out anything interesting?"

"Yes, as a matter of fact. I'm finding out that we better become insiders quick, before it's too late."

A light breeze sent snowflakes dancing, silently pattering against the glass doors, gently begging to share in the warmth that beckoned just inside as they went back to their reading. The wind howled, then whispered softly against the roof, but neither of them seemed to notice.

Two hours later they dressed and went down to dinner. The Inn was famous for its New York steaks, and Merrily was eager to try one. They were following the waiter to a table for two toward the back, when someone called to them.

Turning, Merrily bumped right into Helga Gerber and a blushing young man with freckles and a red neck. "Oh! Sorry," Merrily said automatically.

For an instant she felt stunned, suspended in time; weightless. Then it all came together with a sudden fury. A mounting rage set in with all its complications. Only one question surfaced. What was Helga doing there?

CHAPTER 11

"I HAD NO IDEA that the two of you would be here." Garth glanced across the table, first to Rick and then to Helga. "Here in Berchtesgaden and staying at the same hotel, too." He paused and twisted in his chair, apparently to study Merrily, and directed his next words to her in that deep resonant voice that always stirred her. "It's quite a coincidence. Isn't it, Honey?"

She kept her eyes fastened on her plate and said nothing. But as usual, his sensuous voice touched her.

"It sure was a coincidence for me, sir." Rick rubbed his scalp in a boyish, slightly self-conscious gesture. "I didn't know where you and Mrs. Butler were going. But Helga here . . ." Rick glanced longingly at the blonde beauty beside him and patted the top of her hand, "she wanted to come here."

"I would have thought a young twosome like you and Helga would want something with a little more glamor, like the General Walker for instance, up on

162

the hill." Garth's voice held an outward calm, but Merrily sensed an undertone of hostility. "What made you decide to come here?"

Rick's gaze wandered to Helga again. "Helga said it had to be here," he explained with a smile that Helga returned halfheartedly. "She's the boss, you know."

Garth faked a laugh and turned back to Merrily with a teasingly mocking grin. "I have that same problem. Don't I, dear?"

But Merrily refused to meet his eyes.

"I'd heard of this place for years," Helga explained. "It's quite famous, you know."

"So I've heard." Garth's black eyes caressed Merrily, his lips trembling with a hint of passion. "And just right for *our* . . . purposes."

Merrily had avoided answering or looking at anyone since Helga insisted that she and Garth share their table for four. Inwardly she'd fumed, at least at first, while managing to keep a low, congenial profile. Yet suddenly the fact that she and Garth were at their honeymoon hideaway and eating with Rick and Helga took on, for her, an unrealistic, almost comical air. Or did the situation only seem funny because she was fighting so hard to pretend that nothing was bothering her? *Garth could always have said no,* she reminded herself.

She'd folded and unfolded the napkin on her lap at least a hundred times. Now she suffered from the strong urge to get up and do something, maybe help the waiter clean off the empty tables. Anything. She couldn't continue to merely sit there and do nothing.

Merrily bit her lower lip pensively and tried to concentrate on her steak. She successfully tuned out all conversation at the table, however. Therefore she was at a loss to know how to answer when a question was suddenly directed to her.

"Is that all right with you, Hon?" Garth asked, touching the top of her hand exactly as Rick had touched Helga's. "What do you say?"

"I say fine," Merrily answered, faking comprehension. "Whatever you want." Her blue gaze lingered on her husband's face. Finally, she glanced down at her plate again.

Garth chuckled under his breath. "Now there's an offer I don't intend to refuse."

Merrily looked up, wide-eyed. "What offer?"

"The one you just made." He laughed again. "You said something to the effect that you'd do whatever I wanted."

"Good," Rick put in as if he were unaware of the dialogue going on between Garth and Merrily. "Then it's settled."

Merrily was dying to know what had been settled, but was too stubborn to ask. Instead, she cut a bite of steak and chewed slowly. "This is good." She cut another slice, stabbed it with her fork, and pretended to offer it to the group. "In fact, excellent, I'd say. I read about this hotel in *The Explorer,* a travel magazine I subscribe to, and it's everything I expected."

Merrily's gaze caught Helga's. The blonde beauty looked dazzling in the surprisingly conservative, black jump suit she was wearing. She got the impression that every man in the room was watching Helga also. Was she jealous of Helga's youthful charms? She glanced down at her own torso. Still in the white sweater and matching pants she'd worn earlier, she felt and looked presentable. Garth had indicated earlier that she looked smashing. But she felt commonplace beside the fair-haired Helga.

Garth wore a splashy red ski sweater with navy and white threads dancing through it in a zigzag pattern. He easily outshone Rick in his white dress shirt. Rick also wore an old high school letter jacket

164

that read *Broadland Bobcats* in blue with white letters across the front, drawing undue attention to his youth and lack of maturity.

Garth's virile vibrancy also projected an image of youthfulness, but of an entirely different kind. A stray curl fell across his forehead, softening his tall, commanding presence with a touch of almost boyish charm. She could throttle him for being so handsome. As angry as she was, Merrily still found herself wanting to run her fingers through his dark hair. If that wasn't a sure sign that she was hooked on the man, nothing was. Maybe he didn't know that Rick and Helga planned to be at this hotel this weekend. She should certainly give him the chance to present his side of the story. Or was she merely making excuses for him because she didn't want to believe anything negative about him?

"What time shall we meet then?" Rick asked.

"Meet?" Merrily's blue eyes questioned, her musical voice literally hanging in midair. "What do you mean, meet?"

"The four of us," Rick continued. "We're meeting for bridge in our room later. We just talked about it."

"Bridge," she faked. "Oh sure. As I said, whatever all of you decide is fine."

Rick's eyes never left Helga's face for an instant as he said, "Eight-thirty all right?"

"Sure. Eight-thirty's fine." Merrily glanced at Garth. "Okay?"

"Sounds good as far as I'm concerned."

She hated the way he said that, as if playing bridge was the most exciting thing he could think of. It was supposed to be their honeymoon after all. Wasn't being alone together the whole idea in coming?

"But I'm not sure about Merrily," Garth said with

a sympathetic glance to his wife. "She hasn't been feeling well, I'm afraid. Maybe it would be better if we refused after all."

Liar, she thought. Why was he trying to pin the refusal on her? "But I'm feeling fine now," Merrily blurted a little too sweetly. "Really, dear. I feel just great."

With clenched jaws, Garth glanced out the window at the falling snow, then back at Merrily with a hooded expression that only Merrily unmasked. "With the weather this way, I suppose a nice stroll downtown is out for this evening anyway. But that's no problem since Merrily enjoys reading." His dark eyes mocked her.

"Lately, I read the Bible," Helga put in innocently.

Well, Merrily thought, ignoring Helga's out-of-character comment. *So you want to play rough do you, Garth?* Merrily concentrated on her steak again as if she hadn't even noticed his eyes. "Bridge is probably the best idea I've heard all day."

How's that for a put down, Cap'un? she thought. She could read his displeasure by the angry glint in his eyes. The nonverbal communication between them was quite stimulating.

"If we unite our efforts and keep our foursome together," Rick pointed out, "we can have a nice vacation here in spite of the storm."

Tongue in cheek, Merrily kept her eyes lowered to keep from laughing. "You're absolutely right, Rick. Our foursome should try to be together as often as humanly possible . . . keep each other from being bored. After all, there are just so many things you can do during a snowstorm and especially without the benefit of a working television set." She glanced away in mock despair and shrugged. "Right, hon?"

"Right." He shot her an "I wish I could strangle

you" look and began sawing his baked potato as if it was a piece of tough steak . . . or possibly her neck.

"Enjoying your meal, dear?" Merrily asked innocently.

Garth glared at her a moment before taking a bite of potato. "Tremendously. And you?"

"I'm having the time of my life, and it's all so . . . enlightening. Don't you think?" Merrily faked an air of thoughtfulness. "Now let me see. What else could we all do together?" Merrily's eyes never left Garth's. Therefore, she got to see him almost choke on his potato. "Careful, *darling*. I'd hate to see you choke and miss the bridge party." She paused and handed him her glass of water. "Here. Try this."

His scathing glare blazed above his glass as he drank.

Merrily glanced away dismissively and smiled. "So much for choking. So where were we? Oh, yes. Now what else can we all do together?"

"Helga and I were planning a side tour to Salsburg, Austria, in the morning if the roads clear up," Rick related eagerly. "You two could come along."

"Great!" Merrily gloried in Garth's thinly veiled displeasure. The thought of still another foursome activity would enrage him, making it all the more appealing. Her blue eyes laughed at Garth with a trace of challenge. "Isn't this fun?"

His eyes shouted, *no,* in the strongest nonverbal communication she'd seen yet. He didn't want to go with Helga and Rick to Salsburg; maybe he didn't want to play bridge. But he'd started this disgusting foursome thing by agreeing to share their table, and she was going to play it for all it was worth.

"I know of some historic churches in Salsburg that Inga told me about," Helga put in. "Maybe we could all go there tomorrow."

"Lovely!" Merrily exclaimed, pretending elation. "You have such good ideas, Helga." She turned to Garth. "Doesn't she, honey?"

He frowned painfully.

"I know what!" Merrily's eyes alighted with still another mock glow of enthusiasm. "Let's make Helga the social director of our little group. She could plan all of our activities while we're here. All the rest of us would have to do is sit back and enjoy."

Merrily glanced back at Garth again. The look he returned made her think of the word *throttle* and see an image of her own throat with his big hands around it. Smiling slyly, she went on. "Now let me think."

Merrily paused, as if in deep thought, watching her handsome husband with amusement. It was all she could do to contain herself. A belly laugh was just below the surface. She could feel it. And the effort required to hold it in was becoming more impossible all the time.

"Garth always rises early at home," Merrily went on. "So I'm sure he wouldn't mind if you started our organized activities early, Helga." She paused again. "Say." She glanced down at her watch. "How does 6:30 sound to you?"

"In the morning?" Garth exploded.

"Or did you want to rise even earlier, dear? Would 5:30 be better?"

"You're out of your mind, Merrily. This is supposed to be a vacation, not field maneuvers for land sakes."

"I know." Merrily's voice was laced with mock compassion. "But with Helga's help, I'm sure we can make it almost as exciting."

Seemingly unaware of Merrily's barb, Rick cut in. "I know Helga's willing to try to plan our outings in the best way possible, aren't you honey?''

Helga smiled sweetly at the lovesick Rick, and
then glanced at Merrily with a warm, almost friendly
expression that was baffling. The German beauty
was full of surprises. "I'd be glad to try," Helga
said softly, and Merrily almost believed she meant it.

"That's all anyone could ask for," Merrily continued, still playing her game to the hilt. But somehow
Helga wasn't reading her lines correctly. She was
suppose to be the villianess. "Imagine a young
couple like Rick and Helga wanting to spend time
with an . . . an *old* couple like us.''

"You're not old, Mrs. Butler," Rick insisted defensively. "And Captain Butler isn't either.''

Merrily glanced back at Garth with pretended pity
and touched his hand tenderly. "You wouldn't think
so, would you?''

Rick, she noticed, was all but swimming in Helga's green eyes. He'd hardly taken his eyes off her
since they sat down at the table.

"Garth holds his age well, I think," Merrily went
on. "Another Ronald Reagan, I'd say. It's really
quite remarkable.''

Garth glared at her. "Well thanks a lot, sport. You
hold your age well, too, I might add. Considering.''

"You're too kind." She glanced challengingly at
Helga. "In fact," she paused dreamily, "I think I'll
keep him.''

"I hope you can." Helga shrugged meaningfully.
"All any of us can do is study God's Word and
pray." She glanced hopefully at Rick. "I mean the
divorce rate is . . .''

"Staggering," Merrily said for her. "But for me,
marriage is a lifelong commitment.''

"And for me as well," Helga said, still gazing directly at Rick.

Stunned, Merrily watched in silence as Helga

reached out and took hold of Rick's hand. *What kind of game was Helga playing?* she pondered. Or had she changed? Helga was beginning to sound like Shelly.

Helga turned and smiled at Garth. "And what about you, Captain Butler? Is marriage, for you, a lifelong commitment also?"

"Of course."

"Even when it's nothing more than a meaningless title?"

Garth cleared his throat nervously. "Well, of course, there are times, within a marriage, when insurmountable problems make continuing . . ."

"Unwise?" Helga completed for him in a soft, asking voice. "Or maybe you meant to use the word *impossible*. I know exactly what you're probably thinking because I used to feel . . ."

"What I intended to say was that so-called insurmountable problems never come up in my . . . in our marriage." Garth stared coldly at Helga. "Merrily and I work out our problems like two sensible adults."

Do we? Merrily asked herself. Or was Garth merely pretending, playing a game with himself?

Suddenly the playful mood she'd been in earlier lost its luster. Merrily had only one desire: to leave that table for four immediately and run to the refuge of their room on the second floor as fast as possible.

Merrily bit her lower lip. "I'm sorry. But all at once I'm really not feeling well. If all of you will excuse me, I think I'll go upstairs now."

Garth got to his feet. "I think I'll turn in too."

"No use spoiling your evening," Merrily pointed out. "Why don't you stay here with your . . . our friends and enjoy yourself?"

"Yes," Helga agreed eagerly. "Why don't you, Captain Butler? And let me attend to Mrs. Butler.

Sometimes a woman's touch can be very helpful.''

Garth looked down at Helga from his towering height with a bored, slightly disgusted expression. ''That's quite impossible,'' he said with a note of finality. ''My wife is ill, and I must attend to her. And under the circumstances, the bridge game is off as well as the trip to Salsburg.'' With that, he put one huge hand to Merrily's slender back, guided her to the cashier's counter, then out the door, and up the stairs.

Rick and Helga were downstairs in the coffee shop the next morning when Helga got a headache and went back to their room for a bottle of aspirin. Their room was directly across the hall from the Butler's. But she wasn't thinking of them. Helga locked their room after she came in and was in the bathroom when she heard someone unlock the door. At first she thought it was Rick. Who else could it be? Then she remembered that she had their only key.

Afraid even to breathe, Helga crept to the bathroom door and carefully peered out. A slim blonde girl of about sixteen surveyed the contents of Helga's purse with obvious interest.

''Just what do you think you're doing?'' Helga demanded in German. The young girl gasped, then froze, dropping the purse on the brown carpet.

Helga moved forward. The fear she'd first felt was replaced by an air of power. She could see fear in the girl's pale, bluegray eyes and sense the inner trembling. ''What is your name and what are you doing with my purse?'' Helga demanded.

''I'm Gretel Bauer, the cleaning girl.'' The girl's voice was shaky, and she spoke in her native German. ''I saw some loose change on the bed, and I was putting it back in your purse for safekeeping.''

''Who would believe such a story?'' Helga insisted

171

coldly. "It's your word against mine."

"But it's the truth, I swear." Gretel's pleading tone softened Helga's expression but only slightly. "I could lose my job here," Gretel exclaimed. "And I support not only myself but my younger brother. Have mercy, please! We are orphans."

"That's unfortunate. But you should have thought of that before you tried to rob me."

"But I wasn't robbing you, Frau. You must believe me."

Helga paused, appraising the panic she saw in the young girl's eyes. Her Lord would want her to forgive Gretel. "I believe you, and I will not report the robbery." With a rush of memories, Helga recalled Mark Knight's picture that she needed to return. "But would you be so kind as to do a small favor for me?"

"Anything!" Gretel reached down for her purse, then handed it to Helga.

"There's a photograph, a small wrapped package, and a letter there on the table." Helga glanced toward the lamp table by the bed. "I want you to deliver them to Room 228 across the hall when the guests are out. This should be easy for you to do since you will be cleaning the room sometime today anyway."

Gretel got the package and other objects that Helga mentioned without a backward glance, then turned back to Helga. "And where in the room would you wish me to put these objects?"

"Oh." Helga paused thoughtfully. "Anywhere where they are sure to find them. Maybe on the bed."

"Very good. Is that all you would have me do?"

"Yes, thank you. That is quite enough." Helga smiled then, and the trembling girl relaxed. "You see my husband and I are checking out this morning.

172

If this were not so, I'd do the chore myself. We will be going to America soon, and we have a lot of planning to do.'' Helga's smile widened as she handed Gretel a small roll of German marks from the purse she'd been clutching nervously. "Please agree to take this. It's a gift to you. My Lord, Jesus Christ, would want you to have it.''

"You are very kind.''

"No, Gretel; it's Jesus who is kind, and He loves you very much.''

Surprised but happy, Gretel left Helga's room and hurried downstairs.

Sometime later that same morning, Gretel Bauer watched from the shadows as Garth and Merrily disappeared into the elevator. She crept out then into the dimly lit hall, pulled out a silver ring filled with an assortment of keys, and opened Room 228. Quietly, she slipped inside and shut the door.

The Butlers were in a gay mood as hand in hand they left the crowded hotel. At a city park several blocks away, they set about the task of building a rather large snowman. Or they thought it was big until a bigger one began to take shape only a few feet from them. The other builders were a group of rosy cheeked children in cheery red or green knit caps and brightly colored woolen coats. They were completely absorbed in their work and didn't appear to notice Garth or Merrily.

However, Merrily was drawn to a young boy of about ten or so who appeared reluctant to join the others. He stood slightly away from the rest. He was part of them, and then he wasn't. Her heart reached out to him. Before she knew it, she was at his side, asking him to help build the snowman she and Garth had started and hoping he understood English.

"I know it's not as big as the one *they* are build-

173

ing," Merrily pointed out disparagingly and glanced toward the competition. "But with your help, I know we could make it just as attractive."

The boy was motionless for a moment. Then he nodded and almost smiled. "I have seen you at the hotel," he added at last. "You were kind to those who served your table. I will help you make the man from snow."

"Do you live there?" Garth asked.

"My sister is a maid at the hotel, and we live in the cellar."

"Where are your parents?" Merrily put in.

The boy stiffened. "They died of a fever a few months ago."

"And you have no other relatives to help take care of you?" Merrily's heart was reaching out again, and she didn't even want to pull it back. "None at all?"

"Only my sister Gretel . . . and our grandparents in Frankfurt."

"Why don't you go and stay with them?" Merrily suggested candidly.

Garth shot her a warning glance. *This is none of our business, Merrily,* his eyes said. *Just stay out of it.*

I will not! she thought boldly. *There's no way I'll stay out of it.* "I saw how young the maid they call Gretel is, when we first checked in. Is she your sister?"

He nodded.

"Would you like to go to live with your grandparents?"

"Oh, yes. And we will go when Gretel has saved enough money for our fare on the train."

"Garth." There was a begging expression in the large, blue eyes. "Can we?"

"When you look like that, I can hardly refuse."

174

He paused. "But not right now. This minute. I want to check things out a little first."

Merrily's eyes bubbled with excitement. "Oh, you're so good. So kind. Thank you." She smiled down at the boy then. "By the way, what's your name, future snowman builder?"

The boy returned her smile. "I am Johann. Johann Bauer."

"Welcome, Johann Bauer," Garth said warmly and extended his hand. "We can really use your help."

The boy took his hand and smiled back at him. Then he appeared to put all his energies into completing a rather lopsided snowman.

By the time the snowman was completed, Johann had agreed to take his supper that night in the dining room at the hotel with Merrily and Garth, and Gretel was invited, too. Of course she accepted. But Gretel was forced to leave their table early because she had some household chores that couldn't wait back at the tiny, cellar apartment she shared with her brother. Johann stayed and chatted with Garth and Merrily quite some time, however. He even ended up telling them the details of their rather desperate financial needs. Garth and Merrily offered to help.

But it was not until he got to their apartment that Johann was able to share their good fortune with his older sister.

Grinning widely, Johann's round-cheeked face radiated enthusiasm as he hurried to his sister's side on the couch. "We have no need to wait even one day to leave this place!" he said. "Herr Butler has offered to buy our tickets to Frankfurt tomorrow morning."

"No, Johann," Gretel insisted firmly. "We cannot take charity from strangers. I will buy our tickets on the train."

"But what if you cannot save enough before Bruno gets back? I will be back in school by then and who will save you from the beast?"

"You have no need to worry. I will have the money in plenty of time. I did some extra work for a married lady who was a guest here in the hotel. With that and the money I make here, we'll make out, I'm sure."

"It is good that you had an extra job, Gretel. But I would rather take the money Herr Butler is offering and leave tomorrow."

"No. We can't, little brother. It was kind of them to offer, but we will be unable to accept."

Merrily couldn't stop talking about Gretel and Johann for the rest of the evening. They were so young and helpless. She sensed that something was terribly wrong. If only Gretel would agree to let them help. Garth had said that it was none of their business. But she knew that deep down, he was as concerned as she was. Gretel and Johann were simply too young to live alone as they did. And Merrily had seen the lewd looks the manager gave Gretel when he thought nobody was looking.

That was why Merrily felt so hopeless when Johann informed her later that same evening that Gretel would not accept their offer of help. From looking at the boy, she knew that he was holding something back. If Garth had been with her, she couldn't even have asked Johann her next question. Garth would never have allowed it. But he'd gone to a newsstand nearby for an evening newspaper. Therefore, she felt free to say what she liked.

Merrily put her hand on Johann's shoulder compassionately. "What's wrong? Please tell me, so I can help you. And don't say it's nothing because I know you're holding something back." She gazed

176

deeper. "Trust me, Johann. Please!"

"I cannot tell you. Gretel would be angry."

"She'll never know. I promise."

He glanced away worriedly for a long moment, then looked at Merrily squarely in the eyes. "You promise?"

"Yes."

"Very well then." He paused and gave a deep, reluctant sigh. "There is a wicked man named Bruno who was a guest recently at this hotel. He made several unseemly advances toward my sister while he was here. She was able to avoid them, but now he's coming back in just two weeks. I'll be back in school by then and can be of no help to her." He hesitated again as if afraid to go on. "But she has a good job working here at the hotel. That should bring her the money we need for our journey to Frankfurt. You've been very kind but you don't need to worry about us anymore. Soon we'll be far away from here and under the care of our grandparents. Nevertheless, we appreciated your friendship and kindness to us."

"Johann," Merrily said just above a whisper. "Please let me give you the money you'll need anyway. It will be our secret." She saw the doubt in his young eyes. "Then should Gretel come up with the money you need, you can mail me back our money when you get to Frankfurt," Merrily went on. "But if you need it, to get away from Bruno, you'll have it. Okay?"

The doubt increased to a slow shake of his sandy-haired head. "My sister would not be pleased. I'm sorry."

"It's only a loan. Nothing more. I'll expect to be reimbursed. I'll give you my card with my name and address on it. Now what can be wrong with that?" She'd already gotten out her card and was slowly

177

counting out the money as they talked. "Here's my card and the money you'll need plus a little extra for food along the way. And when you pay back the money, I'll expect one mark more for the interest on the loan just as any bank would require. Isn't that fair?"

He slowly nodded.

"As you can see," she said, "I'm not doing this purely out of concern for your welfare. For me, it's a business deal as much as anything else. Would you rob me of the chance to make a little extra money?"

Johann shook his head again. "Oh no! I would never want to do that after you've been so very kind to us."

"Then take the money as I asked you to do. Okay?"

"Very well then," Johann said reluctantly. "I will do as you ask."

Sickened at the thought of some disgusting man attacking poor little Gretel, Merrily turned away toward the coffee shop, leaving Johann behind.

Merrily felt no better when she joined Garth later. She'd gotten the boy to accept the money, but had no intentions of telling Garth exactly how she'd managed to do it. She knew she'd end up telling him about Bruno though.

As Merrily prepared for bed that night, she was still silent. Reflective. Unresponsive to Garth's many attempts at conversation. She'd been like that all evening. So far, she hadn't spilled the story about Bruno. But she didn't know how much longer she could hold out. She ached to share the burden she felt. Horrible mental pictures of Bruno, what he must be like, kept flashing before her.

She *had* to help Gretel and Johann. From what she'd learned of the Lord through Shelly, God would want her to. Suddenly she realized that Shelly's sermons were getting through somehow. When had it happened? Was Shelly right after all? Was a personal relationship with the Lord the missing ingredient in their shaky marriage? With a frown, she squelched the thought.

Garth appraised his wife's recent behavior thoughtfully. Something was definitely bothering Merrily. Was she remembering her honeymoon with Mark Knight? Comparing him with Mark? Something happened to change her. The physical side of their relationship had gone from a perfect ten to zero since breakfast that morning. He could almost think his presence disgusted her. Once when he tried to hold her close, she pulled away and said, "Is that all men ever think about?" He needed to get to the bottom of her sudden withdrawal. But his pride wouldn't allow it.

"Is something wrong?" Garth asked finally as gently as he could manage. "You look so strange tonight."

"Thanks a lot."

Her sharp retort hacked him. "You're welcome, I'm sure." He tried to smile. "Would you like to go out on the terrace for a while?"

"It's freezing outside. Do you want me to take my death?"

"No. I want you to take two aspirins and try to calm down. Maybe get something to read."

"You sound like Shelly. She reads Billy Graham. Maybe I should read Doctor Spock. This baby of yours makes me nauseous."

Why was she attacking their child? Did she hate it, too? "Are you sorry because you're having our child?" Garth asked coldly. "Is that it?"

"No. Of course not." She looked at him as if she had no idea what he was talking about. "I love my babies as soon as I know they exist inside me. You know that."

But you loved Mark's babies more, he thought.

"What does my pregnancy have to do with anything?" She was thoughtful for a moment. "You're upset about what I said about the baby making me sick. And now you think I don't want the baby. Well, you're wrong. I love kids. And all unborn babies make their mothers nauseous. I don't even know why I said that. When I'm pregnant, I say all sorts of crazy things." She glanced over at the bed, then started toward it. "I'm sorry. I guess I'm just tired." She yawned, stretched, and turned down the covers. "Think I'll turn in and finish that book Shelly made me promise I'd read."

"There's no couch available in here that I can see," Garth said with leashed fury. "So I have no choice but to sleep with you." He hated the expression of distaste that flashed briefly from behind her eyes before he climbed in bed beside her. "Of course, there's always the chance that I can rent an extra room."

"That won't be necessary, I don't think."

"You're very kind." His eyes sparked with telling indignation on hearing her bored response, but his voice still held a measure of control. Slowly, he tried to relax, then noticed that Merrily was tossing and turning on her side. "What's wrong now? You're tossing and turning like some kind of . . ."

"You'd wiggle too if you had a pillow as hard as mine."

He reached for her. But his hand hit something hard, under her pillow. "What's this?" With his free hand, he flipped on the lamp, pulling out something slick and square with the other.

Even in the dim light, it was plain that he held a photograph, *the* photograph, the missing picture of Mark Knight hidden under Merrily's pillow. Stunned, he stared down at it in silent unbelief as if it were some foreign object that someone brought back from outer space or something. He didn't notice that Merrily was staring, too.

"How could you, Garth?" Her mental gasp was almost audible. "This is . . . it's unforgivable!"

"What is?" he demanded. "Finding out about your little secret?" His voice was too calm, too slicing to be interpreted as anything but what it was . . . a cold, bitter assault. She'd gone too far this time, much too far. "How long have you been sleeping with Mark's picture under your pillow, Merrily? Was it there on our wedding night?"

CHAPTER 12

"WELL, WAS IT?" Garth persisted.

Merrily's lips quivered, a mild hint of the devastating blow his words did to her bruised psyche. She couldn't even speak. To him, that was probably a sure sign that she was guilty-as-charged. But she wasn't. How could he suggest such a thing? She had no idea how Mark's missing picture ended up under her pillow. *Unless Garth put it there.*

Slowly the thought began to swell, gain strength. Who else could have done it? They kept their room locked. Even Helga wasn't a suspect this time. The idea that Garth had any part in it was repugnant. She felt a sick pulling in the pit of her stomach.

She knew that Garth was jealous of her late husband; maybe he hated him. But this? It was lower than anything she ever thought he'd stoop to, lower even than taking the picture in the first place. She wanted to fade away; die. Disappear completely.

"Why don't you answer me, Merrily?" His voice was deep and coldly biting. "Was *his* picture under your pillow on the night you became my wife?"

The hurt was there again, in his eyes. But there was something else, too, a horror that went beyond rage. She was almost afraid to answer.

"Are you refusing to answer because the answer's yes?"

He took hold of both her shoulders and shook them with a grip that was stronger than anything she'd ever experienced before. And a new kind of fear engulfed her.

"Answer me!" he shouted. "I'm tired of this! And I'm warning you. Things are going to change around here. Or else!"

"You're hurting me! Let me go!"

"Not until you tell me the truth!"

His dark expression terrified her. "Please Garth! You're really hurting me!"

The inner turmoil etched in his handsome face lasted a moment longer, and then he slowly relaxed. Somehow, her pleading voice, her horror-filled eyes, got through to him. In his crazed furor, he obviously hadn't realized the potency of his own strength, that he was actually hurting her physically. When he did, he froze, loosening his iron grip but not releasing her entirely.

Amazed and ashamed, Garth merely stared down at her for a moment, unable to put into words the repentant ache that tore at his heart. He forgot why he was angry or that she'd never answered him. His entire mind cried out against the pain he'd caused her with one voice, one aim: To make amends. Yet at first, no words came.

Like a man drowning, he pulled her to him then, held her firmly yet gently, and buried his face in the dark softness of her long, near-black hair. "Forgive me," he begged. "I never meant to hurt you! I wasn't thinking. I must be mad, crazy, or something." He pulled down the straps of her blue silk nightgown and began to kiss the red finger marks, so apparent against the softness of her smooth creamy skin, with quick butterfly kisses. "Please, say you forgive me. You know I'd never intentionally hurt you. You are my darling, my sweet Rachel. I adore you, love."

At the height of his most passionate display ever, at the word *love*, a warning bell went off inside his smitten brain. Everything with him was suddenly pulled back, like a jumbo-jet braking to a belated halt. Brakes screeching, he released her and carefully pulled up her drooping gown straps. "I can't take back the physical hurt I've caused you, Merrily, by merely saying that I'm sorry. I really wish I could . . . that it was that simple. But I can make sure that you're not bothered by more of the same. Therefore, I think I'll go downstairs and see if there are any extra rooms available in the hotel."

He hesitated, waiting for some kind of response from her. *Anything* would be better than the frozen stare she was giving him at that moment. "I think we should check out of this place in the morning," he added. "We only hurt each other here, it seems."

Dazed, Merrily watched in silence as Garth charged from the room wearing only a pair of blue cotton pajama bottoms and his black terry-cloth slippers. At any other time she would have laughed out loud at the ridiculousness of his scanty attire. There was a raging snowstorm outside. It was cold in their room even with the fire; it was probably near freezing out in the hall. But at that moment she was too numb to notice anything. Even the loud bang when he slammed the door didn't break the trance-like stupor his previous actions conjured.

She could have, should have said something, done something when she had the chance. Why had she merely recoiled there on the bed like some mindless snail?

With a sudden rush of adrenalin, Merrily compelled herself to move, react, and a flood of blinding fury possessed her. *I hate him*, she thought, yet all the time she knew in her heart that she didn't, couldn't. But that didn't mean that their marriage wasn't falling apart. In fact from the looks of things, it had already fallen.

She had to do something, make some kind of plan regarding her future and the future of her children. Cross-legged in the middle of the bed, she tried to think. Obviously she could no longer depend on her marriage as a power base. She'd dreamed too long the impossible dream, the one that always included Garth. *It's past time to embark on a new dream*, she thought, squeezing her balled fists nervously. *I need to take charge of my own emotional life—with or without Garth Butler.*

Without him. The thought stuck in her brain as if it was welded there. How could she live without him now that she'd known the sweet enchantment of his kisses, the tender rapture of his love? Even now she longed to feel his arms holding her.

Still the anguish, the inner pain, persisted. If Garth actually took Mark's picture only to torment her with it later on, he was . . . No! He couldn't have done such a thing. There had to be another explanation.

Emotionally as well as physically exhausted, Merrily fell back against her pillow again and was astonished to find that it still felt hard, like a very smooth rock. She rolled over on her stomach automatically with a sort of subconscious fear of the unknown and cautiously reached under her pillow. With a start, she felt something. But it was several heart-stopping seconds before she had the nerve to remove that something and see what it was. A neatly wrapped, white package stared back at her, and she had the oddest feeling that she was holding a time-bomb or something equally as deadly. Then she noticed that a white envelope was attached to the package. Scolding herself for her lack of bravery, she decided to open it.

With a hopeless sigh, Merrily ripped open the envelope and pulled out a handwritten letter addressed to her and Garth.

Dear Captain and Mrs. Butler,

How do you ask for forgiveness when your sin (or in my case, sins) are so horrible as to be almost unforgiveable? I say almost because I am hoping that you can and will forgive me. What I am saying is, I stole the picture of Mr. Knight in hopes of causing problems in your marriage. I did a lot of other things, too, and all for the same reason. I am not the same person I was three weeks ago. That Helga does not exist anymore.

That was what I intended to tell you, had you two come to our room to play bridge or agreed to go sightseeing with us. But since that did not happen, I am forced to write you instead. By the time you read this, Rick and I will have checked out of the hotel and be well on our way back to Volksheim, assuming that the trains are able to get through after the heavy snowfall. Otherwise, we will still be here but at a different hotel. I really think that is best, don't you?

Your friend, Shelly Trenton, gave me a lot of good advice a few weeks ago, and she also gave me a Bible. And that wonderful old book, the Holy Bible, has changed my life. I couldn't believe how relevant it was to today's problems. It seemed impossible since I knew that it was written ages and ages ago. But it was and is for today, I found out, and it has certainly helped me. Now, instead of wanting to leave my husband, I want nothing more than to

186

serve my Lord, Jesus Christ, for the rest of my days as the wife of Rick Webber. That is quite a change for me. I do not understand it all yet. I am learning though.

But to make a long story short, I am returning Mr. Knight's photograph, and I would like you to accept as a gift from me a Bible that is identical to the Bible that Shelly gave me. It is my earnest hope that you too can find the peace and love that I have found in Jesus Christ. I will be praying for you always.

Love in Jesus Christ,

Mrs. Helga Webber

Perplexed, Merrily put down the letter and opened the package. A large-print King James Bible fell out and into her hands. Inside, the inscription read, *To Captain and Mrs. Butler. May the joy of the Lord bind you each to the other in Christian love, and may your marriage last a lifetime. With much love, Rick and Helga Webber.*

Garth shivered in a darkened linen closet to the right of their room and down the hall. He'd been there since his hasty departure, and was now contemplating how he could return without losing face. He'd covered his near naked body with every available sheet in sight, but it did little against the numbing cold. He was beginning to wonder if saving face was all that important considering the alternative.

When he finally did go back to their room, wrapped from head to toe in white, freshly ironed sheets, he couldn't have been more surprised. Merrily was propped up in bed reading, of all things, the Bible.

"I thought hotel room Bibles were peculiar to the United States." There was a cutting tone in the deep, throaty voice. "I had no idea the Gideon

Society had infiltrated Germany, too."

Pretending to ignore him, Merrily continued to search the index for the word *Rachel*. She had a sudden urge to read the story of Jacob and Rachel for herself but had no idea where to find it in the Bible. It only annoyed her more when Garth wandered over to her side of the bed, turning his head at an angle in order to see what she was reading.

"Reading the index, I see." He laughed caustically. "Well, I suppose that's as good a place to start as any." Shivering, he turned to the nearby dresser and began digging for his pajama top. "But if you'll tell me what you're looking for, I might be able to help," he added and laughed again.

"You know the Bible?" She laughed with a sarcasm that topped his. "Ha! That's about as believable as if you told me Ted Kennedy turned Republican."

He was buttoning his pajama shirt when he whirled back around. "Contrary to your obvious opinion of me, Merrily," his eyes challenged, "I have a good knowledge of the Bible thanks to a very caring uncle who happens to love me. But, of course, that's something else that would be hard for you to believe."

"What would?"

"That someone could possibly love me."

She could see him draw within himself as soon as he said those words, trying to hide the hurt. But she'd seen it in his eyes again, loud and clear, and she wanted to reach out.

"Would you help me find what I'm looking for in the Bible, Garth?" she asked softly, her eyes asking for forgiveness. "I'm at a loss to know where to find that Bible story you once told me, the one about Jacob and Rachel."

He smiled suddenly as if what she'd said pleased

188

him. "It's in the Book of Genesis. That's the first book of the Bible. But I'd have to have a look at your Bible a minute in order to find the chapter it's in." He winked teasingly. "I'm good but not *that* good."

She returned his smile and handed him the book. "And almost as modest as you are knowledgeable, I might add."

"Flattering remarks will get you nowhere."

Her eyes twinkled. "But surely it's worth a try."

He was still grinning as he opened the Bible to the first page, then stopped and frowned. "What's this supposed to mean? To Captain and Mrs. Butler. May the joy of the Lord . . ." He frowned at Merrily. "Where did you get this?"

"From under my pillow. It was there along with Mark's picture and a letter of apology. It seems that Helga is responsible for taking Mark's picture." She handed him the letter. "But now she's changed. And she really sounds different in the letter. I'm inclined to believe her."

"She also sounds like a first-rate religious fanatic if you ask me. I'm always skeptical of those quick, personality-change artists. It sounds a little fishy, I think." He paused and shrugged, then began searching for the verses she wanted. "But time will tell, I guess."

"Yes, I suppose so," she said as he handed her back the letter.

When the story of Rachel was finally found, Garth began to read to her directly from the Bible in that deep, heart-touching voice of his. And something strange happened. Something quite remarkable. In those brief moments, Merrily had never felt closer to him . . . and to God.

Since Helga and Rick were no longer at the hotel

and the mystery of Mark's picture was finally solved, Garth and Merrily stayed on as they'd originally planned. They skied, went sledding, and shopping. They even took a side trip, by bus, to nearby Salsburg, and they made love. Merrily also read the Bible regularly for the first time in her life. Often, she found Garth reading it, too. They really needed two Bibles now.

Garth didn't know of Merrily's growing closeness to the Lord. She never spoke of it. Yet it was there. Understanding and a desire to know more burst forth from deep within. Was this the thing that had been missing from their marriage? Was this the substance they lacked?

She read and studied the Bible daily and prayed all during the day . . . when she thought to do it. Mentally, she praised the Lord for everything, not merely for her food. She thanked the Lord and gave Him the glory for *all* her accomplishments and blessings.

As soon as they arrived back in Volksheim, they drove directly to Shelly's to pick up the children. Todd and Suzan bubbled with news and excitement on the drive home. Merrily was also pleased to find a letter from her parents in the mail. Prince Disgusting croaked happily from inside Todd's pocket. He too was glad to be home.

And Merrily felt a lump in her throat when Todd asked Garth to go with him to the Dad and Son banquet at the base chapel that Saturday night.

"I sure would like you to be there, Uncle Garth," Todd said. "And would you mind if I called you Dad just for that one night? It sure would be great, if you don't mind, that is."

"I'd be honored, Todd, to go with you to the Dad and Son Banquet. And I'd like it just fine if both you and Suzan called me Dad *all* the time." Garth tried to hide the emotion he was apparently feeling on hearing Todd's words. But Merrily saw.

"Okay . . . Dad," Todd said, a little self-consciously. "I'll call you that all the time, if it's really okay. Gosh, that's like really having a dad. I mean . . ." He paused and looked up at Merrily questioningly. "I mean, it's like having two dads."

"I think having two dads is just great, Todd." Merrily gazed lovingly at Garth. "And there aren't two better dad's in the whole wide world, I'll bet."

Garth watched Merrily follow Todd and Suzan up the stairs to tuck them in their beds. With a sigh, he sank onto an overstuffed, brown arm chair and rested his feet on the matching ottoman. He was deeply moved by Todd's request that he be called Dad and Merrily's positive reaction to it. What would Merrily say if he told her he wanted to adopt them? He'd even insisted that Mark's picture be returned to its former place on the small table in the children's room. He squelched the thought that Merrily never once mentioned *his* picture.

He could remember well how he'd longed as a child to have just one small photograph of his real mother and how Monique had refused him, scolded him for merely considering such a notion. He'd been a selfish, jealous fool about Mark's picture. A real jerk. Yet, he still couldn't believe that Merrily loved him. Nor was he completely satisfied with the results of their Bavarian holiday. They still weren't as close as they could be.

He loved her so much. Now he loved Todd and Suzan as if they were his own. Maybe, in her way, Merrily loved him. But something was lacking in their marriage, that missing link that his uncle used to talk about.

Merrily reclined in the middle of their big bed and

was filing her fingernails when Garth slipped into their bedroom to join her. He stepped out of his boots and was about to remove his clothes and climb in beside her when he suddenly realized how thirsty he was.

He hated the thought of going back downstairs as he groped under the bed for his slippers. His hand felt something soft, much softer than the terry cloth slippers. He pulled out the soft object and smiled when he saw that it was the baby pillow Merrily had showed him when she told him about her pregnancy.

With pretended anger he said, "Merrily! When was the last time you cleaned under our bed?"

"Three months ago last Tuesday, I believe." Her eyes twinkled teasingly. "Or was it four months ago? I'm sorry, I simply can't remember." She noticed the pillow. "Oh, you found it. How nice. I don't think I ever did remember to send poor Steve a thank you note."

"Steve?" A measure of jealousy flickered, but he managed to hide it. He was determined to give their marriage a chance.

"Steve was the one who gave us the baby pillow."

"Oh, yes. That must have been the same day he kissed you while I laid up here in bed with the chicken pox." His expression had changed from playful to a sort of restrained mockery. "But would you mind telling me how Steve knew about our child before I did?"

"I'm not sure." She paused thoughtfully. "I guess Lilly Arkin or her husband must have told him. She saw me as I was leaving the infirmary and guessed why I was there."

"So the Arkins knew, too. Would you mind telling me who else knew before I did? It's a wonder I didn't find out by reading about it in *The Stars and Stripes*."

"I didn't tell Lilly or Shelly or anybody. They all guessed. You would have noticed, too, if you'd looked at me once in a while."

"Why didn't you look at that photograph I mailed you before we married?" Hurt surfaced. "Is my face so depressing you couldn't display it?"

"What picture? I never got a photograph of you, and it hurt, too, since I mailed you mine."

He felt pleasantly relieved. "You never got the photo I mailed?"

"Don't you know if I had, I'd have written and thanked you?"

He smiled. "Yes. Knowing you, I guess you would have."

She reached out both arms, asking him to hold her. "Now, are we going to let missing pictures and baby pillows spoil our first night home? Or are we going to forget the past and concentrate on the future?" She gave him a teasingly southern, come-hither look. "I'd take a chance on the future if I were you, Cap'un Butler, honey. Why with Miss Scarlet gone and all . . . who knows what mischief we might get ourselves into?"

The southern belle routine worked like a charm. Soon Merrily was in his arms. All thoughts of Steve's gift and missing photographs vanished.

They made love again the next morning. Compellingly. Gloriously. Garth had never been more tender, more loving. Later, he kissed her in the doorway on their way down to breakfast for two in their cheery kitchen. Snow plopped against the hall window pane above the stairs, but all Merrily could hear was her pounding heart. Certainly she never experienced the stirring she felt with Garth in Mark's arms.

Poor Mark. She'd given him so little of herself. Or was it possible that Mark never guessed how she really felt?

"Oh, Mark, I love you so," she blurted out as Garth swooped down to kiss her again.

She'd wanted to tell Garth that she loved him for such a long time, and it finally slipped out. So why did Garth stiffen on hearing it? Why did he suddenly pull away?

"Well!" he exclaimed, pushing her away. "At least we know now, don't we? You don't have to pretend anymore because it's all out in the open."

"What's out in the open?"

"Your feelings!"

"What are you talking about?"

"You finally said what you've been thinking since our wedding night. You finally told me who you love, who you've always loved. But I'll have to hand it to you, Merrily. You're a darn good actress. I was almost beginning to believe you."

"Will you please calm down and tell me what I said?"

He was already out the door. But he turned back and glared at her with such agony that she wanted to cry out in pain. "You finally named the man you love. You said and I quote, 'Oh, Mark, I love you so.'"

With that he stormed across the hall and headed for the stairs with Merrily right behind him. He started down, tripped on a skate that had been left on the stairs, and tumbled the rest of the way.

With a string of mumbled expletives, he picked himself up off the floor, glared one last time at Merrily, and stormed toward the front door, his heavy coat over one broad shoulder. She barely noticed when he pulled a Bible from the pocket of his coat and tossed it on the coffee table on his way out.

She heard the motor rumble to life and a loud screech as he roared out of the garage and down the street.

Pale and too empty to cry, Merrily ran back to her room and fell across their bed. The children would be waking soon and wondering where Garth had gone. It was Saturday, and he'd promised to take them for a drive that morning. Of course, the banquet that night was out now, and Todd would be crushed without his . . .

Dad. Garth seemed pleased when Todd called him that, and she'd been pleased, too. So why did she have to mess up and call him *Mark* of all things? It was hard to believe that she'd actually done it. But she knew she had. Didn't he remember that she was always calling people by the wrong name? Calling Helga, *Inga,* calling Uncle Ted *Uncle Tom* . . . or something equally as stupid.

Once, before she came to Germany, she remembered calling her mother *Suzan.* Because of her problem with names, she'd always hated introducing people. But what did any of that matter now? She'd made the ultimate foul up, and the result would be the total destruction of her marriage. There was no use pretending otherwise. Garth could and had forgiven a lot, but he'd never forgive this. He'd never believe that it was all a horrible mistake.

She had to get away from the house, go someplace where she could be alone. Merrily and the children would have to leave Germany as soon as possible. She had no idea how to go about telling them. *Polly,* she thought. Maybe Polly could help her out . . . at least this morning while the pain was so great.

Without thinking, she picked up the phone and dialed Polly's number. It was awfully early, but Polly was a good sport once she was awake and going. The problem was waking her.

"Hello," Polly said sleepily.

"Hello, Polly. Listen. I need you over here right now. No questions asked. Okay? I want you to keep the kids for a couple of hours, and I want to borrow your car, that is if it's okay with Bob. I think I'd like to take a drive, maybe as far as Wertheim."

"Anything's okay with Bob as long as he gets to sleep in on Saturday morning, and he's still snoring away. So I'll leave him a note and be right over."

"Thanks, Polly, you're a pal."

"And a very sleepy one I might add. We went out last night. Is it okay with you if I crash on the extra cot in the kids' room until they wake up?"

"Sure." Her voice broke. "Just as long as you get up when they do."

"Are you crying?"

Merrily sniffed loudly. "Me?"

"Yes, you!"

"Well." Her voice broke again. "In a way, I guess I am."

"I'll be right over!"

Merrily heard her slam down the phone before she had time to say goodbye. And Polly was banging on her front door before Merrily had changed out of her nightgown.

Fifteen minutes later, Merrily was behind the wheel of Polly's VW and following the Main River toward Wurzburg. She didn't know why she chose that road except that that was the route Garth took on their first drive the day they went on a picnic, and she wanted to go to their hill once more before leaving Germany forever.

They'd stopped several times along the way to sightsee, on *that* day in late July. But she didn't want to stop unless she absolutely had to on this ominous occasion. It was as if she were writing the final chapter to a tragic Shakespearean drama.

The car flew down the wet, icy highway. Everything outside whipped by in a white blur of snowy sameness. She was frantically praying even faster. If she didn't slow down, she was sure to have an accident, and she didn't want that even if everything around her was falling apart. With God's help she and Todd and Suzan and the new baby inside her would manage somehow. With God's help. When had she begun to look to the Lord for strength and guidance? She almost smiled because the thought pleased her. She could always go into teaching. *God willing*, she thought, slowing to avoid an ice-filled hole.

Merrily braked a little too abruptly. The car skidded to one side. Frozen with fear, she counted it a blessing as well as a warning and wheeled carefully out onto the road again. *Thank you, Lord*, she prayed. *And please bring Garth back to me. I love him so. But if you can't, I'll understand.*

At Wurzburg, she was sobbing so hard she could barely see; she almost missed the turn-off to Wertheim entirely. The Main River followed the highway closely from that point on. Soon she would reach *their* hill. From the top of it she'd be able to see the merger where the Main and Tauber rivers united.

At one time she and Garth had united there also. But now . . . Her throat tightened. Why was she torturing herself like this? She wasn't his Rachel. She'd only been kidding herself to ever think she could be. She was Leah, the one he married but never loved.

At last she stopped, pulled the VW to a halt near the spot where they'd parked on that wonderful day. Slowly she began her climb to the top. Moving, lifting one booted foot after the other, gave some relief from the emotional trauma going on inside her. At least now she had something to do to keep her from thinking so much. And it helped but only slightly.

The view from the top was different now. A layer of snow like white, sugar icing covered the roofs of the gingerbread houses. The trees were bleak and bare. Summer had left their magic valley, perhaps never to return.

Merrily bowed her head in silent prayer to the God of Abraham, Isaac, and Jacob. In that moment of surrender, she gave her heart, her mind, and her soul to the King of Kings and Lord of Lords as millions had done before her. And she knew, somehow, that if she'd been the only person that ever lived Jesus would still have died to save her. He loved her that much.

With a soft little cry of emotion she turned, preparing to return to Polly's borrowed car. No doubt Polly and Bob would be wanting it, perhaps to find a hill of their own.

Her eyes were downcast. The only sound was the crunch, crunch of her heavy boots on the new fallen snow. Then suddenly there was another sound, a heavier crunch on the snow. She glanced up and saw . . . Garth. He'd come, followed her. She didn't know how or why. She only knew he was there.

There was a nervous silence with each looking, measuring the other. If he dared say something nasty or funny at that moment, she'd strangle him. But he didn't. He just moved toward her, his dark eyes never leaving hers. Then he took her in his arms and kissed her. His lips felt cold but warm, too, a welcomed sensation.

"I was wrong," he said at last.

"No, I was."

"Are we going to start the second phase of our marriage by arguing about who was in the wrong?"

She shook her head and smiled.

"Good." He grinned at her. "Because I have a

much better idea. And I hope you won't think I'm nuts or crazy or that I've flipped my wig or something. But I want us to pray together, here on our hill. I know we've never done anything like that before. And if I'd seen someone else doing it, even a week ago, I'd probably have called them fanatics. But my uncle once reminded me that the word *fan* is short for *fanatic*. So I guess deep down, I'm a Jesus fan, though I've hidden it pretty well for most of my life." He paused, gazing down at her, "I've given my heart to the Lord, Merrily; I'm . . . I'm a new creature now like the Bible says."

He paused again, waiting for her to say something. But she was speechless, too touched to talk or even breathe. There was nothing she wanted more at that moment than to pray there on their hill with her husband, to renew their wedding vows, dedicate their lives. Yet she was so caught up with emotion, she couldn't utter a word. So she nodded . . . and nodded . . . and kept on nodding until finally he got the message.

He took her hand in his then, and they bowed their heads.

"Heavenly Father, you joined us to each other some months ago in a chapel with a minister and flowers and all the trappings. You bound us together forever then, and we didn't even bother to thank you. Later when the problems set in, we tried to solve them ourselves. But I think we both know now that we can't because you were always meant to be the link that binds us. And without you, we're lost.

"Please become the missing link in our marriage, oh, Lord, and in our lives as you were always meant to be. Forgive us for all our past and future sins. And at the same time know that we forgive those who have wronged us. Thank you, Lord, for sending us Helga and through her, the Bible, your

Holy Word. Thank you for loving us enough to punish us when we need it so that we can learn from our mistakes. Thank you for giving me my Rachel as you gave Jacob his.'' There was a break in his deep, vibrant voice, and Garth hesitated a moment and swallowed before continuing, ''And thank you, Lord, for loving us enough to send your only Son, Jesus Christ, to die for our sins so that we might live and get to know you.

''In Jesus' name. Amen.''

''Amen,'' Merrily echoed and looked at Garth only a moment before falling into his waiting arms. ''I love you, Garth.''

''And I love you, my darling Merrily.''

Just as she had, Garth had found the missing something in their marriage and in their lives. And she knew, as he kissed her, that this was for always.

ABOUT THE AUTHOR

A native Texan, Molly Noble Bull lives with her husband Charlie and their three sons on the Texas Gulf Coast. *For Always*, her first novel, placed second, statewide, in a general novel contest in 1984. Though fiction, the German setting comes from her memories of a time, some years ago, when Charlie was stationed in West Germany with the U.S. Army. The Bull's shared an old, two-story, German house, then, with their life-long friends, Frank and MaryKay Schwerthoffer of upstate New York. Together, the adventure began.

A Letter To Our Readers

Dear Reader:

In order that we might better contribute to your reading enjoyment, we would appreciate your taking a few minutes to respond to the following questions and return to:

Editor, Serenade Books
The Zondervan Publishing House
1415 Lake Drive, S.E.
Grand Rapids, Michigan 49506

1. Did you enjoy reading FOR ALWAYS?

   ☐ Very much. I would like to see more books by this author!
   ☐ Moderately
   ☐ I would have enjoyed it more if _____

2. Where did you purchase this book? _____

3. What influenced your decision to purchase this book?

   ☐ Cover   ☐ Back cover copy
   ☐ Title   ☐ Friends
   ☐ Publicity   ☐ Other _____

4. Would you be interested in reading other Serenade/ Serenata or Serenade/Saga Books?

   ☐ Very interested
   ☐ Moderately interested
   ☐ Not interested

5. Please indicate your age range:

   ☐ Under 18   ☐ 25–34   ☐ 46–55
   ☐ 18–24   ☐ 35–45   ☐ Over 55

6. Would you be interested in a Serenade book club? If so, please give us your name and address:

   Name _____

   Occupation _____

   Address _____

   City _____ State _____ Zip _____

Serenade Saga books are inspirational romances in historical settings, designed to bring you a joyful, heart-lifting reading experience.

Serenade Saga books available in your local book store:

Serenade Serenata books are inspirational romances in contemporary settings, designed to bring you a joyful, heart-lifting reading experience.

Serenade Serenata books available in your local bookstore:

Watch for other books in both the *Serenade Saga* (historical) and *Serenade Serenata* (contemporary) series coming soon.